# RISEN FROM ASHES

## HONOR & DUTY BOOK 6

### SAM SCHALL

*For my family.*

*They pushed her too far.*
*Now she's coming for them.*

# BATTLE CRY

1

_____

ONE WEEK. Seven days spent praying enemy reinforcements didn't arrive. Seven days of every medically able member of the taskforce working nearly around the clock to bring at least some of their ships back up to battle readiness. Seven days spent wondering if their target would find a way out of the system before they moved in and made an arrest.

And seven very long days for her guilt to grow.

But, for the first time in those seven days, anger surpassed guilt and she embraced it. If there was any justice in the universe, their quarry would give her reason to kill him. Preferably slowly and painfully. It might not bring the dead back, but at least she'd be able to tell their families the man responsible had been made to pay for what he did.

"Secure the exits," she ordered as she stepped off the lift. As she did, the other fire teams reported in, confirming they were in place and no one could reach the floor without her permission.

Colonel Ashlyn Shaw watched as four battle armored Marines moved into position, two remaining at the lifts and the others moving to the far end of the corridor. A bitter smile twisted Ash's lips as the sounds of their boots striking the marble floor filled the air. She waited, wondering if their quarry would appear to investigate the strange sounds. But no. Either he was too much of a coward or he didn't believe they'd dare come for him on his own turf. Not that it mattered. Soon enough she'd have him in custody. One way or the other, he would face justice for his betrayal of the taskforce, a betrayal that cost so many deaths.

"Exits secure, Angel."

She glanced at the Marine standing next to her, his battle rifle in hand, and nodded. "Clear the floor, Shadow. I want it quick and quiet."

"Roger that, Angel."

It didn't take long. Less than five minutes passed when word came that the last office on the floor had been cleared. Only three had been occupied. No one offered any resistance. More importantly, the workers had been quick to confirm their target was in the meeting room at the far end of the corridor.

"Ranger, Goru, you have our *guests*," she commed. "Thumper, shut down the lifts." She waited for confirmation. "Let's move in."

Weapons at the ready, nine of Fuercon's best Marines, moved purposefully down the corridor toward their target. As they took up positions near the meeting room doors, Ash nodded. She watched as one of them scanned the area beyond the wall. A moment later, Ash pulled the image up on her HUD and studied it. Six people, all sitting around a table in the center of the room. None of the scans showed active security and only two of those present appeared to be armed.

"On my mark."

A hand on her arm stopped her as she took a step forward. Eyes flashing, not that her Marines could see with her faceplate darkened, she glanced at the Marine who'd been her shadow the last few days. Sergeant Michael Shaw shook his head. Then he activated a private comm link.

4

"Angel, no. Let the heavy armor make entry first."

She ground her teeth in frustration. She'd known it had been a mistake to bring him. He knew her too well. Unfortunately, Admiral Collins left her little choice. It was bring her younger brother, currently assigned to her team after the death Master Gunnery Sergeant Kevin Talbot and others under her command, or remain on the ship.

"This is my mission, Shadow."

"And you are the regiment's CO," he reminded her. "Angel, we can't risk you," he added softly. "Your Marines need you. Don't make them grieve for you as well."

She closed her eyes and counted to ten. Leave it to him to know exactly what buttons to push to guilt her into doing as he wanted. "We will discuss this later."

He gave a nod and stepped back. Without waiting for permission, he signaled the two heavy armored Marines to take their positions at the door. The others fell back, weapons at the ready.

"Blow the door. Concussion grenades to follow," Ash ordered as she pulled her battle rifle from the scabbard across her back.

"Roger that, Angel," Boomer, the team's explosives expert, replied.

From her place down the corridor, Ashlyn watched as the man set the charge at the double doors. A moment later, he gave a thumbs-up. He and his partner, Rogue, moved to either side of the doors. Every Marine watched as Boomer lifted his right hand, all five fingers visible. One by one, a finger lowered, marking the countdown to detonation.

The controlled blast blew the security locks from the door. Before the smoke cleared, the heavy armored Marines moved into place. Rogue kicked open the doors. Boomer tossed in a concussion grenade. Ash nodded as the cries of surprise at the initial explosion turned into something else. Pain and disorientation replaced the surprise and anger. If she had her way, that would soon turn to fear.

"Move in!" she ordered.

The Marines moved as one. This was a maneuver they'd practiced until they could do it in their sleep. Less than sixty seconds later, six members of the Savitar VI government were secured and on their knees at the rear of the room. Behind each one stood a Devil Dog. The six wouldn't be going anywhere without Ash's permission.

And, as far as she was concerned, they could all go to Hell. Unfortunately, that wasn't her call. Not unless they did something she could point to as justifying the use of deadly force. She might be willing to risk her own career, but she would not put the careers, much less the lives, of those under her command in jeopardy just because she needed to avenge the deaths of Talbot and those onboard the shuttle with him.

"It's your show now, Angel," her brother said softly over their private link.

"We're still going to have that talk once we return to the ship, little brother." She reached up and touched the side of her helmet. Her face plate turned transparent. "Let's do this."

She scanned the room, noting not only where her Marines and their prisoners were but any potential sources of danger their scans might have missed. Satisfied there were no unexpected surprises awaiting them, she crossed the room. She reached out with a gloved hand and she tilted up the middle man's face so she could look him in the eye.

"Name!" she barked out in her best parade ground voice.

"How dare you!" He struggled to stand, only to find himself easily held in place by the Marine behind him.

"Your name."

"Governor Charles Edward Fonteneau and I'll have your commission for this."

Ash reached up and removed her helmet. Her brother stepped forward and took it from her. As he tucked it under one arm so his gun hand remained unencumbered, she nodded to the Marine behind Fonteneau. Without warning, Strider pulled the man to his feet.

"For the record, I am Colonel Ashlyn Shaw, 7thDivision 10thRegimen Fuerconese Marine Corps," Ash said even though Fonteneau knew exactly who she was. They'd been in communication before and after the Callusian attack. But Admiral Richard Collins, the taskforce's

6

commanding officer, wanted this done by the book. "Charles Edward Fonteneau, it is my duty to inform you that you are now in the custody of the Fuerconese Navy. The transitional government of the Savitar VI System met, heard the evidence against you and granted my government's request to take you into custody."

She reached out and her brother handed her a datapad. She glanced at the display, not that she needed it to remind her what the charges were against the man. Holding his gaze, she read off the charges, pausing briefly after each one. Let him wonder if that was the last charge or if there were more to come.

"You will be transported to Taskforce Avenger. From there you will be taken to Fuercon to answer the charges against you. Once you have, it is possible you may be returned here to face any charges your home system wishes to bring against you. But, for now, you are ours."

"You can't!" He struggled against the hands holding him. Then he cried out when, after a simple nod from Ash, Strider kicked him in the back of his knees and forced him once more to the floor. "We--" He looked frantically to either side, indicating the others being held by Marines. "—are the government. There is no legitimate provisional government."

"I beg to differ. From my understanding of the system's constitution, the provisional government was duly formed and sworn in. But that's not my concern. I'm sure your counsel will raise that issue once you are on Fuercon." Not that it would do him any good. At least she hoped not.

"Fonteneau, I have one question for you now. Who else worked with you to betray my people?" Fonteneau looked at the floor, refusing to answer. With a sigh, Ashlyn turned to her brother. "Sergeant, assign three Marines to escort this piece of shit back to our shuttle. Make sure he doesn't do so much as stub his toe." She paused, waiting until Fonteneau looked up. "However, if he does anything that could even remotely put the Marines in danger, they aren't to hesitate to use whatever force they feel necessary to contain him."

"Roger that, Colonel." He quickly instructed Strider and two others to do as Ash ordered.

She waited until the three left the room. Then she turned her attention to the others. For several long moments, she studied them. She'd been briefed on each of them. Nothing in the briefing material pointed to them having betrayed the taskforce. Of course, until they intercepted the attempt to hack the system defense platforms, none of them suspected Fonteneau of even considering betraying them to the enemy.

Then there was the fact none of the five had been included in the new provisional government. That could simply be politics, or it could be the newly formed government's way of pointing a finger at them without actually making any accusation. Either way, she needed to determine what role, if any, the five played in Callusians attack on the system. She would not leave the surface until she had everyone responsible for what happened to the taskforce in custody or buried.

"Move them to chairs but do not remove their restraints," she ordered.

Once seated, the three men and two women watched as Ashlyn paced up and down in front of them. The only sounds in the room were those of her boots against the marble floor and their own breathing. It was as if Ashlyn was a jungle cat deciding which of her petrified prey she'd attack first.

"As I told Fonteneau, I am Colonel Ashlyn Shaw, commanding officer of 7thDiv10thReg. My Marines are the ones who dropped to the surface of Shennong to look for survivors. They risked their lives to do what your own military should have been ordered to do. My Marines, along with our naval counterparts, stood ready to protect the system when the Callusian invasionary force returned. We were willing to die to do so. What we did not know was that Fonteneau, and perhaps one or more of you, tried to betray Taskforce Liberator. That betrayal failed but at the cost of more than a thousand Fuerconese and allied lives. Lives we will avenge one way or another."

She let the threat hang in the air for several moments before continuing.

"I have a question and I'm only going to ask it once. If you refuse to answer, or if I have reason to believe you are lying, you will be removed to the flagship and taken to Fuercon to answer the same charges your former system governor faces."

"You don't have the authority," a redheaded woman at the end of the row began.

Ash turned to her, a smile as cold as ice, on her lips. "I have every authority," she corrected. "Admiral Collins informed your Chief Justice of the charges against Fonteneau before our arrival. The Chief Justice, pursuant to your laws, reviewed the evidence and agreed there was more than enough to support our claims. He then convened a meeting between the leaders of the various political parties in the system. They formed a provisional government and reviewed the charges and supporting documentation. Once the Chief Justice signed the appropriate legal documents confirming the charges, the government granted us permission to take Fonteneau and anyone else who might be involved in the conspiracy into custody for removal to Fuercon.

"My question, ladies and gentlemen, is quite simple. Who knew of Fonteneau's plans and why were no steps taken to stop him?"

She watched and waited. The remaining five looked from one to the other. Several looked shell-shocked, not only by the events of the last few minutes but by the revelation of what Fonteneau had done. But two, including the redhead, betrayed themselves. A bland looking man Ash normally wouldn't look at twice swallowed hard and sweat beaded on his upper lip. The redhead jerked once against the hands holding her in place as all color seemed to drain from her face.

That was more than enough for Ash.

"Sergeant, those two are to be taken into custody. Have them escorted to the shuttle."

Her brother quickly did as she said. As the two were taken from the room, Ash leaned against the table, seeming to relax. Even so, her rifle still rested in her hands and the remaining Marines remained on guard.

"You will be held here a short while longer. If you cooperate, you'll receive our thanks and be allowed to return to your families. It will be up to the provisional government to determine what role you play going forward but that's not my concern."

One by one, they nodded in understanding.

"However." Her voice turned hard once again. "If I discover you lied, or if you do anything that could endanger my people, you will find this is your last moment of freedom. Any attempt to harm my people will result in your deaths. Do you understand?"

Each of them swallowed hard once and then nodded. It wouldn't take much more to have them pissing themselves and she didn't care. Let them understand how grave an error they made by not stopping Fonteneau before Talbot and the others were killed.

"We'll cooperate," the remaining woman said. "Majel Karkoc, Interior Ministry."

"Let her up." She watched as Karkoc stood. "Ms. Karkoc, I hope you do. We lost some very good men and women in the attempt to keep the Callusians out of this system. They were our brothers- and sisters-in-arms, something we Marines take very seriously. Any attempt to prevent us from doing our duty here will be dealt with swiftly and without mercy. Do you understand?"

"We do." She glanced at her companions and they agreed.

"Sergeant, I leave it to you to secure the information we need. I'm returning to the shuttle to report to Admiral Collins."

"Aye, Colonel. Corporal Branz will accompany you."

"Updates every half hour, more frequently if needed." She took her helmet from him and once again secured it in place. Then she activated their private link. "Keep comms open, Mike. If there's trouble, get back to the shuttle on the bounce."

"You just watch your six, Ash. We've got this."

She hoped they did. The last thing she wanted to do was tell their parents something happened to him on her watch.

## 2

---

President Derek Harper looked at the half dozen men and women standing around the table. Two wore mess dress uniforms and had braced to attention the moment he entered the room. The others wore business suits and stood, their eyes on him, as they waited for him to speak. Instead, he held them where they were, his expression grim.

"I have two questions." Anger roughened his voice. One hand fisted at his side. In the two years of his presidency, he'd done his best to protect Fuercon and her allies. A large part of that time had been spent rooting out the corruption that sprang up during the previous administrations. Now he found himself fighting against betrayals by supposed allies. "Do we have confirmation of Admiral Collins' accusations against Governor Fonteneau and has the admiral taken that son-of-a-bitch into custody?"

"Mr. President, I'll begin with your second question, if I may." Secretary of Defense Linden Klingsbury waited for Harper's nod of

11

approval before continuing. "Admiral Collins sent Marines under Colonel Shaw's command to take Fonteneau into custody. The mission was successful and the Marines not only arrested Fonteneau but secured evidence against him and several others in his administration. The former governor and two others are currently being held in the brig onboard the taskforce's flagship. They, along with all evidence against them, will be transported here as soon as their relief is on station."

Harper's mouth firmed before he forced himself to relax. Then he sat and motioned for the others to do so as well. As he did, he considered what to ask next.

"Fonteneau's motive? He requested our assistance. So why try to betray the taskforce to the Callusians?" Especially considering how the enemy essentially wiped out the entire population of the planet Shennong with the biotoxin they then attempted to use against the taskforce. The very thought of what would happen to a ship's crew if exposed turned his insides to water.

"Preliminary information from Admiral Collins indicates he did so after the Callusian commander threatened to use the biotoxin against the system's capital planet," Klingsbury said. "It seems Fonteneau's mantra has become 'I did only what I needed to in order to protect my people.'"

Harper nodded. Part of him understood. He'd do almost anything to protect Fuercon and the other planets in the system. But he couldn't forgive the betrayal of his people, not when they'd been in the Savitar VI System at Fonteneau's request.

"And the biotoxin. What do we know about it?"

"Not much more than before, Mr. President," Dr. Imad Tabion, the Navy's chief medical officer, said. "The taskforce's medical teams and researchers have sent their preliminary reports, but the results are, to be honest, incomplete. That isn't a criticism. The labs onboard the ships simply aren't set up for the sort of research needed to do an in-depth study of the biotoxin. In other words, we won't know much more until the taskforce returns and we get our hands on the samples they managed to obtain."

"Then what do we do to protect our ships, our personnel and our planets in the meantime?" That, more than anything else just then, was what mattered.

"For our ships, we follow the steps Admiral Collins and his people instituted," Admiral Miranda Tremayne began from her place down the table. "Compartmental discipline is put into place at all times, not just when the ships are at battle stations. It will be inconvenient, but it is our best bet at limiting exposure if the enemy manages to breach the hull with the biotoxin." She paused, her expression grim.

"Mr. President, my recommendation—and I've already passed it along to Secretary Klingsbury is to take an aggressive approach to challenging any ship nearing our system borders. The same should be done by any of our forward elements. It might cause some hurt feelings, but I'd rather have that than dead crews."

Harper glanced at Klingsbury who nodded in agreement. "Issue the order. Any ship refusing to identify and allow boarding is to be turned back. If they refuse, they get one warning shot across the bow. After that, if they fail to comply, the consequences are on their CO's heads.

"Ladies and gentlemen, we are now in a defensive position where the home system is concerned. We will remain so until we have a better handle on what's happening." Something they should have been doing anyway. They knew the Callusians would do whatever it took to defeat them and their allies.

"Yes, sir," the others replied.

"Now, what about our Marines?" Harper turned his attention to the dark-skinned, grim-faced woman sitting midway down the table.

"The armorers are already working on refining the additional filters and seals Colonel Shaw's Marines used on the mission. The tech gurus are working with the medicals to update armor sensors to detect the biotoxin. That is the best we can do with our current equipment until we know more about the biotoxin and how it works." General Helen Okafor, Commandant of the Fuerconese Marine Corps, glanced at her datapad before continuing. "Mr. President, the real key is going to be decon procedures to get the Marines from the surface—or from onboard infected ships—to their own ships without undue delay. The procedures Taskforce Liberator put into place will work, but there must be a way to shorten the length of time needed to run through decon without putting a ship's company at risk. Once the taskforce returns and the researchers have time to breakdown the biotoxin, our people will work with them not only with regard to our armor but the decon procedures as well. Captain Dalton said it best: 'we can't do shit until we know exactly what we're working against.'"

Harper's lips twitched slightly. He knew the Corps' chief armorer. The man was as irascible as he was devoted to keeping his fellow Marines safe.

"My people are in full agreement with Dalton, sir," Dr. Tabion said. "We can do some preliminary work on combating the biotoxin, but until we have samples, our usefulness is limited."

"Then we need to get the taskforce home ASAP."

Everyone around the table nodded grimly.

"But we have to make sure the Savitar VI System is protected when the taskforce pulls out." Fonteneau may have betrayed the taskforce, but Fuercon would not leave the system to the mercy of the Callusians. "Admiral Tremayne? Secretary Klingsbury?"

"Orders have gone out for elements of Fifth Fleet to divert to Savitar VI, Mr. President," Klingsbury said. "The fleet will be supplemented by ships from the Cassius System. Taskforce 57 should be on station in another week. They're under orders to progress there at best military speed."

Harper nodded. "Issue orders to Admiral Collins to bring his ships home as soon as 57 arrives and he's had a chance to brief its commander." He leaned back and thought for a moment. "Will the taskforce be battle ready by the time they depart the system? The last thing we need is for it to fall on its way back here."

"I'm sending a squadron out to act as escort, Mr. President," Tremayne said. "They will rendezvous with Admiral Collins' ships, hopefully before the taskforce leaves the system. The squadron departs in-" She checked the time.-"Less than an hour. As far as the

14

crews know, they are taking part in a training exercise. They'll be told the truth once on their way."

"Very good, Admiral, and thank you." He closed his eyes and tilted his head back for a moment before sitting up. "I understand you haven't seen all the evidence our people have managed to gather in the Savitar VI System. Based on what you have seen, did Fonteneau ask for help knowing he would betray our people or was this something that happened after the initial call for assistance?"

For a moment, no one said anything. Then General Okafor spoke. "Mr. President, that's a question we don't have an answer for—yet. However, based on reports I've received from Colonel Shaw, I believe Fonteneau made the decision to betray our people after he requested our help. The Callusian commander, Navarch Jurah Dadd, was one of the most vicious of their COs we've dealt with. Our people, Navy and Marine alike, never managed to defeat him before Savitar VI. That is mainly because he tended to sweep into a system, destroy its defense and comms platforms and then lay waste to the system before allied forces could respond. We know his people have not only stripped planets of their resources but have taken prisoners, selling them into slavery. His reputation for ruthlessness was confirmed by what he did to Shennong."

"But?" Harper asked.

"My guess, and it is only a guess until the taskforce returns home and we have a chance to review everything they discovered, Dadd's mission was specific this time. He was to deploy the biotoxin against a secondary planet in the system. Doing so accomplished at least two things. First, it allowed the Callusian high command to evaluate the biotoxin's effectiveness. If they'd used it before now, we'd have heard of it, even if they did so against a planet they already held. This sort of mass murder isn't something that can be kept quiet for long.

"The second thing the mission accomplished was that it put the fear of God into the rest of the system. I have no doubt Dadd then played on it. Whether he laid out a plan for Fonteneau to lure allied ships to the system or he somehow managed to contact the former governor after Taskforce Liberator's arrival, we don't know. But

15

Fonteneau has been consistent in one thing: he continues to claim he acted as he did to prevent Dadd from turning the capital planet into a wasteland. It doesn't excuse what he did, either to his own people or to ours, but Colonel Shaw believes him."

Harper nodded, his expression grim. "What else?"

"Dadd's death leaves a gaping hole in the Callusian Navy's command structure. More than that, it takes a major player out of the picture. We need to find a way to take advantage of it before someone steps into his place."

"Helen's right, sir, on several levels," Tremayne said. "Had it not been for the sacrifice of the Marines on the shuttle that intercepted the missile targeting the flagship and the inspired battle plans put together by Admiral Collins and Colonel Shaw, the system would have been lost and we'd never know of Fonteneau's betrayal. More importantly, we wouldn't know the enemy has managed to weaponize the biotoxin to be used with their torpedoes. But all that pales in the face of Dadd's death. We've bought ourselves and our allies some time to put new defenses into place and to press our advantage with the enemy."

"What can we expect from the Callusians in response to what happened in Savitar VI?"

"Fleet Intel is split, Mr. President," Klingsbury admitted. "Most feel the enemy will continue with its current operations while trying to fill the void left by Dadd's defeat. A few feel the enemy will make a quick strike on a new target, most likely utilizing the biotoxin, to keep allied forces off-balance. That would buy them time to find someone to fill Dadd's place in the command structure."

Harper considered both options. "Let's pray for the former but plan for the latter. Send word to our allies about our plans concerning system defense. No details, just philosophy. Let's not risk the messages falling into enemy hands. Tell our representatives onsite more details will be forthcoming via courier."

He stood, his expression thoughtful. When the others made to follow suit, he waved them down. "Helen, I want a more visible presence outside the Midlothian embassy. Coordinate with capitol security. We have no evidence Midlothian knew or took part in what happened in Savitar VI, but let's not take any chances. Most of all, let's not take a chance that they've managed to smuggle samples of the biotoxin on planet. No one goes in or out without being checked."

"You know the ambassador will protest," Secretary of State Marc Nelms said, speaking for the first time.

"Let him." Harper started to say something else. Then he blew out a breath and relented. "If he does, remind him that we have more than enough proof that members of his government plotted with the Callusians against our interests and the interests of our true allies. Either he allows the searches or he packs up his staff and their dependents and they all leave Fuercon on the first transport off-planet."

Nelms made a quick note before slipping his datapad into a jacket pocket.

"I want one thing made perfectly clear not only to the Midlothians but to everyone." Harper leaned forward, hands on the tabletop, eyes flashing. "Fuercon will no longer be at the mercy of so-called allies working behind the scenes to harm us. Marc, draw up the appropriate communiques to the Midlothian government and our representatives there. They are to hand over everything they have on Alexander Watchman and those who worked with him against our best interests. Those we have identified as part of the conspiracy are to be arrested within seventy-two hours of receiving the communique and handed over to our representative for transport here to face charges. Failure to do so will be taken as an act of war and dealt with accordingly.

"A similar message is to be sent with the taskforce heading out to relieve Taskforce Liberator. If Savitar VI wants our assistance, they will fully cooperate with the investigation, no hesitation and no attempts to hide anything from our people. Failure to comply will mean a complete withdrawal of all allied ships in the system and a cessation of allied aid in any form.

"Ladies and gentlemen, Fuercon will, first and foremost, do everything necessary to protect its citizens and interests. Our next obligation is to our allies, those who have stood with us against the Callusian threat. But to accomplish that, we must take the fight to the

Callusians and end this war once and for all. The first step to doing so is moving our ships into position to launch the final strike. The second step is to find out everything we can about the biotoxin and how to protect our people from it. If any of you are not fully onboard with me on this, I will accept your resignations now. Otherwise, you have work to do." He pinned each of them with a firm look. One by one, they stood and even the civilians braced to attention and assured him they were with him. Good.

"We will meet again in two days. I want updates morning and evening until then."

With that, he turned and left the conference room. As he did, he hoped they had time to regroup and adapt not only their tactics but their equipment to the Callusians' latest threat. Otherwise, the war would end, but not in the way he wanted.

---

*Fuerconese Taskforce Avenger*
*Savitar VI System*

"Ma'am, are you sure there's nothing else I can do for you?"

Ashlyn shook her head without looking up from her report. No one could get her what she wanted: Talbot and the others back safe and sound. They'd died trying to shield the taskforce, specifically the flagship. Nothing she did or said could change that. They'd died heroes, sacrificing their lives so others could live. Exactly what she expected of all her Marines—what she expected of herself. Not that it made their loss, especially Talbot's, any easier to accept.

"Go get some rest, Corporal. I'm going to finish my report and then do the same."

She listened as Corporal Branz left her quarters. Once the hatch slid shut behind the young man, Ash leaned back with a sigh. Then she stood and crossed the room. A moment later, the sound of whiskey being poured filled the air. She sipped, poured some more and returned to her desk.

Three weeks. Three long weeks since the taskforce came so close to destruction thanks to Fonteneau's betrayal. Three weeks while they waited for reinforcements, praying the enemy didn't return first. Three weeks where she'd been unable to truly mourn her dead. The only good to come during that time was Fonteneau's arrest. He'd face Fuercon's justice for what happened, but it wasn't enough. It would never be enough.

Sipping the whiskey, she ordered the screen across the room to activate. A moment later, the image came into focus and she smiled grimly. Every night she watched the same scene, Fonteneau in his cell several decks below. It was the closest Admiral Collins let her get to the man now that he was in custody. Not that she blamed him. Collins knew her well enough to recognize her need for vengeance. Unfortunately. Instead of getting a modicum of satisfaction from Fonteneau, she had to be content with watching him in his cell.

She sipped some more whiskey as she returned to her desk. Two weeks as a prisoner had changed Fonteneau. Gone was the man's bluster. Now he looked beaten. The medical staff warned he might turn suicidal. Hearing it, Ash ordered around the clock monitoring of the man. She wouldn't let him take the coward's way out. He would stand before the bar and face judgment for what he'd done.

She closed her eyes, the whiskey glass dangling from one hand. For a moment, she allowed herself to imagine what it would have been like had her brother not stopped her the morning they took Fonteneau into custody. She'd been prepared to be the first through the door, hoping, praying the former governor tried to resist. She'd have killed him without a second thought.

And Mike knew it. She had no doubt Admiral Collins did as well and that was why he'd made sure her brother was part of the team, even though she was the Marine CO on the mission. Even as resentment rose, deep down she knew they were doing everything they could to protect her and save her career. Not that it helped just then.

Opening her eyes, she watched as Fonteneau pushed off from the bunk where he'd been sitting. He paced the length of his cell, watching the cell door as he did. He might be beaten but he had yet to give up hope that escape was still possible. God, she wanted him to try. More than that, she wanted to be there when he did. That would be her excuse to kill him, preferably very slowly and very painfully.

*Get a grip, Ash. You do that and you're no better than him.*

The need for vengeance burned deep inside. Since her return from the penal colony on Tarsus the previous year and her subsequent pardon, she'd come close on several occasions to losing control. It didn't matter that most of those responsible for all that happened to her and those under her command on the Arterus mission had been brought to justice. They lived while her people had died or had been brought up on charges and sent to the penal colony with her. Worse, they still didn't know exactly how deep the conspiracy ran. FleetIntel and the JAG were still investigating. Ash knew she might never have all the answers about what happened and that rankled her more than she wanted to admit.

But that paled compared to the anger burning through her now. Losing Lucinda Ortega mere months before this mission had come close to breaking her. Ortega had been her best friend, her former XO and her sister in every way but blood. Knowing her death, and the deaths of others under Ortega's command, could have been prevented only made the loss worse. But Ash had been able to do something about what happened. She'd helped expose the incompetency and indifference in Ortega's chain-of-command and those responsible would never again endanger another Marine. Then she'd been able to help defeat the enemy forces responsible for her friend's death. She been able to act and that helped with her grief.

She finished her whiskey and climbed to her feet. As she moved to stand before the screen, her fingers tightened their grip on the glass. What she wouldn't give to have Fonteneau's neck in her grasp. Damn him!

She lifted her glass to her lips and frowned to find it empty. For a moment, she considered pouring herself a second drink.

*Angel, you've had enough.*

A sob caught in her chest. She knew it wasn't him. Talbot was dead, along with the other Marines in the shuttle. But she heard him just the same. Just as she'd heard him every time she started feeling sorry for herself or started thinking about ways to get to Fonteneau.

"Damn it, Loco, why? Why did you have to play the hero?"

Tears stung her eyes. He'd been one of the few constants in her life as a Marine. They served together on the *Heinlein* her first mission out of the Academy. He'd had her back then and later, when they once again served together. When she and the others had been brought up on charges, he'd been one of those fighting to prove her innocence. On that fateful day she'd been given a pardon, he'd been the one to return her dog tags to her. Since that day, they'd served together. He'd been friend and mentor, brother and fellow Marine. Now he was gone and there wasn't a damned thing she could do about it.

*Quit feeling sorry for yourself, Angel. This isn't the sort of Marine you are, and you know it. Now get a grip. Your command deserves your best.*

She could almost see him standing in front of her, expression serious, eyes worried. He'd kept her from doing anything foolish after Tarsus. Now his memory was trying to do the same thing.

God, she needed him now.

No, what she needed was a night where she slept without the ghosts of all those she'd lost, especially him, haunting her. Maybe then she'd be able to think straight.

Besides, Talbot wasn't there. He wasn't speaking to her. That was her subconscious playing tricks on her again. Talbot, along with the others in the shuttle with him, were dead. There was nothing left of them, no bodies, not personal effects except for what they left in their quarters, to return to their loved ones. Those brave men and women had sacrificed themselves to save the flagship and everyone onboard. She needed to push through her grief and do them proud.

But that could wait until tomorrow. She hadn't allowed herself to grieve after Arterus. She hadn't given voice to her anger, much less done anything about it, after her pardon. Since that day, she seemed to move from one potential catastrophe to another. She hadn't had time to catch her breath, much less mourn her losses. If holding it together a little longer meant drinking when she was off-duty, well, she wouldn't be the first commanding officer to do so.

Nor would she be the last.

With one last look at Fonteneau's image, she turned away from the screen. Instead of pouring herself another drink, she put away her glass. It might not have been Talbot, but the memory of him had been right. She owed it to her Marines to hold it together until reinforcements arrived. She owed it to her dead not to let the governor and those like him beat her and lessen their sacrifices.

"All right, Loco. I'll shape up." She hoped. "But I am going to make every damned one of those bastards responsible for what happened to you and your team, to Lucinda, and to our people on Arterus pay."

And heaven help anyone who stood in her way.

---

How had it gone so wrong?

Charles Edward Fonteneau dropped onto the edge of the narrow bunk in the cell he'd occupied since that bitch Shaw and her Marines took him into custody. Despair filled him. He didn't deserve this. He'd done nothing wrong. He'd done what any system governor with a loyalty to his people would do. He'd tried to protect them from even more harm at the hands of the Callusians.

Damn Shaw and damn the Fuerconese!

He lay back and covered his eyes with his arm. He knew they watched him, looking for any sign of weakness they could use against him. To hell with them. He wouldn't give them the satisfaction of breaking him. He'd continue protecting his system, no matter what the cost.

That was the crux of it all. It was what he'd use to fight these ridiculous charges against him. He'd done his duty. He'd already lost one planet in the system to the Callusians. No one, not his intelligence people and not Fuercon and the rest of their so-called allies, had anticipated the use of the biotoxin. That failure cost thousands upon thousands of people their lives and Shennong was interdicted for who knew how long as a result.

He'd tried explaining it to the intelligence officer who interrogated him every day. Every single day. But the man wasn't interested in what he called "excuses".

"Tell me again. Why try to hack the defense platforms when the Callusians returned to the system?" Captain Julian Galloway asked the previous day.

Just as he'd asked every other day. The phrasing might be different, but the import of the question was always the same. Just as his answer was.

"It was the only way to keep my system safe."

Why wouldn't they believe him?

Perhaps they didn't care. After all, it wasn't Fuercon or any of its allied planets facing the threat of the biotoxin. He knew what the Callusians were capable of. Navarch Dadd made it clear he wouldn't hesitate to use the biotoxin against the capital planet. His duty as system governor was to prevent another massacre from happening. If that meant sacrificing the Fuerconese taskforce, he would.

And he'd do it again.

Now he was the one in custody and not the cowards in the government who refused to do more than wait for the taskforce to come save them. He'd done what he could to prevent millions more of his people from dying. What were a few thousand deaths compared to millions?

"What would you have done had you known about the precautions Admiral Collins put in place to protect the system?" Galloway asked during the last interrogation session.

There had been no answer. Fonteneau knew better than to say "exactly what I did" or words to that effect. Had he known, he would have revealed it to the Callusians. Unfortunately, the last thing he'd expected was for the Fuerconese to keep him in the dark. They'd not only locked him out of the system's defense platforms, but they'd installed other platforms he hadn't known about. The moment he saw those secondary platforms go online, he'd panicked. He knew Dadd would carry through with his threat to destroy the system and he was helpless to prevent it.

Unless he found a way to subvert the taskforce's precautions.

Goddammit! He'd done everything for the sake of his people. Why couldn't they understand that?

"On your feet, Fonteneau!"

His stomach pitched and he swallowed hard. With no option but to comply, he sat up and then stood. As he did, the color drained from his face. Two armed and armored Marines stood at the hatch to his cell. Each day, they appeared like clockwork to escort him to the interview room for the next interrogation session. Not once had they said anything more than what was required to move him from point A to point B. Today would be no different, so he made no attempt to engage them.

A short time later, he sat at the table in the center of the interrogation room. His right wrist was secured to the table. Not that he had anywhere to go if he were able to get free from the room.

Get free! What a laugh! The door was secured. Two Marines, armed Marines, stood guard. And he was on a fucking spaceship. Where the hell could he run?

And what more did they think he could tell them?

The hatch slid open and he blinked in surprise. For the first time since his capture, Captain Galloway wasn't alone. A Marine, a non-com if he correctly identified the insignia on the man's light armor, entered just behind the intel officer. Something about the Marine's expression sent a chill of fear down Fonteneau's spine. Had they decided their hands-off approach to interrogation was no longer working and the Marine was there to extract the information in a more direct manner? What if they'd decided he was no longer of any use to them?

Oh, God, was this it?

"Charles Edward Fonteneau, this is Sergeant Michael Shaw, Fuerconese Marine Corps. Sergeant, you had something to tell the prisoner?" Captain Galloway said from the other side of the table.

Shaw stepped forward until he stood next to Galloway. His dark eyes flashed, his expression hard, he nodded once.

"Charles Edward Fonteneau, I have been tasked with informing you that you will be transferred to the custody of Fuercon's Naval Intelligence Agency upon our arrival in the home system. There you will be formally charged with crimes against Fuercon and her allies. You will be brought to trial. If you are convicted, you will serve out your term at a penal colony under Fuercon's control. Once your term has ended, you will be returned to Savitar VI to face any charges they wish to file against you.

"Much as it pains me because your actions cost the lives of a number of good men and women, I have also been tasked with giving you one last chance to cooperate." Shaw's expression left no doubt that he'd much rather shove him out an airlock than deal with him. "Failure to do so will be taken as bad faith on your part and will noted during your trial. Cooperation will be considered to help mitigate your crimes."

Shaw leaned across the table in his direction. Fonteneau swallowed hard and pulled back as far as he could. Fear licked at the edges of his control as the Marine's gaze bored into him.

"Personally, I want you to refuse. I want Captain Galloway to look the other direction so I can escort you to our Marine CO for a little *chat*. You are responsible for the deaths of your people on Shennong because you failed to insure adequate defenses for the system. You are directly responsible for the deaths of every member of Taskforce Liberator who sacrificed themselves to save your system. Far as I'm concerned, you're nothing more than a fucking traitor to Savitar VI and an enemy combatant to Fuercon and her allies. So please, refuse to cooperate and give me a reason to deal with you in a very permanent manner. It will give me great pleasure to save my homeworld the expense and trouble of trying you."

Bile rose in Fonteneau's throat and he swallowed against it. When he looked to Galloway, hoping the captain would call Shaw off, he moaned softly. The intel officer, instead of ordering the Marine to back down, appeared to be studying something on his datapad. There would be no help from that quarter.

"Y-you can't."

"I can and I will." Shaw straightened and one gloved hand fisted at his side. "Either answer the captain's questions or come with me."

Left unsaid was "please come with me."

"What do you want to know?"

Fonteneau dropped his head into his hands, sinking into despair. This was a nightmare he'd never wake up from. All he could do was try to stay alive long enough for his government to negotiate his return. Those still in power surely worried about what he might say about them. To save their own skins, they'd get him back from the Fuerconese. They had to. All he had to do was stay alive long enough for it to happen.

"See, Sergeant. I told you he'd be reasonable." Galloway sat up and turned his attention to the prisoner. "Let's start at the beginning. When was the first time the Callusians contacted you?"

# 3

---

ADMIRAL RICHARD COLLINS finished reviewing the latest report from Captain Galloway and leaned back. Under most circumstances, he wouldn't have approved the use of intimidation against a prisoner. At least not one like Fonteneau. But these weren't normal circumstances. The man withheld information that cost an untold number of lives on Shennong and on the system's ships and defense platforms. And that was before he considered his own losses.

And near losses.

Some of those losses weren't from physical injuries. One in particular concerned the admiral. He'd done his best to give her time, understanding the depth of her grief. He'd even seen some improvement, at least when she was on duty. But it wasn't enough. Not when the taskforce was only a day out from Fuercon. The last thing she needed, and the last thing he wanted, was for those not on the mission to see how deeply she'd been impacted by their losses. It was exactly the sort of ammunition her detractors would use against her.

27

Not that he blamed her. Hell, if he was honest with himself, he carried the same guilt Ashlyn did over the deaths of Talbot and the others on the shuttle with him. He also carried the deaths of every Marine and every sailor—he smiled at the ancient word—under his command. Their faces, like the faces of all those who'd died under his command over the years, would haunt him. However, he learned long ago he couldn't let their deaths impact the way he performed his duties. That would be a disservice to those still living and a betrayal to the memory of the dead.

Not that it helped in the dark of night.

It was a lesson he knew Ashlyn learned early in her career. But that was before the events of the last five years. Her own beloved Corps, at least certain members of it, had betrayed her and her command. She'd lost people on Arterus. The survivors had been sentenced to the penal colony on Tarsus with her where they'd had to fight for survival until President Harper pardoned her and began the search for those behind what happened. She hadn't truly recovered from that before a new set of losses hit. First was Colonel Paul Pawlak, the Devil Dogs' former CO and Ash's friend. Only a few months later, Lucinda Ortega, her former XO and sister in every way but blood, died in battle. Now Talbot. The Master Guns had been friend, mentor and, since her pardon, often her anchor, keeping her from doing anything foolish. It was no wonder the young woman was reeling.

Even so, Ash managed to maintain while on duty. She might be closed down emotionally, but so were her Marines. They suffered the loss of their comrades as much as she did. More than that, they knew all she'd been through the last five years. Now they formed a protective buffer between her and anyone or anything that might set her off.

Collins shook his head, a slight smile touching his lips. He had no doubt they would storm the brig and give her a few minutes with Fonteneau if they weren't convinced she'd kick their butts for doing so. Ash might be hurting, but she was still their CO and she wouldn't let them do anything to jeopardize their careers or their freedom. She stood for them just as they did for her.

But the time had come, like it or not, for him to step in and knock some sense into her. Unfortunately, he wasn't sure how.

Five minutes later, Collins stopped outside Ashlyn's quarters. As he did, Sgt. Michael Shaw snapped to attention where he stood in front of the door.

"I need a few minutes of the colonel's time, Sergeant."

"Begging the Admiral's pardon, sir, but Colonel Shaw left instructions that she not be disturbed."

"I understand, Sergeant, but this is important." When Shaw remained where he was, Collins sighed. He understood, but he did not have time for this. "Sgt. Shaw, I'm not here to bust your sister's chops. But I am not going to let her destroy her career and possibly get herself sent back to the penal colony because she's hurting. Hell, son, in her place, I'd be doing everything I could to get to that bastard Fonteneau."

He waited, watching as Shaw considered what he said.

"Sergeant, we are less than a day out of Fuercon. Do you have any idea what your sister's detractors will do if they find out how badly Talbot's death rocked her?"

Shaw swallowed hard and nodded once, his expression hard. Good. With the young man on his side, Collins had a chance of breaking through to Ash. At least he hoped so.

"You remind her of that when she comes for my head, sir." Shaw turned and entered a code on the touchpad next to the door. "Admiral Collins, ma'am," he announced before stepping aside so Collins could enter.

Collins stepped inside and waited as the hatch slid shut behind him. Ash stood across the room, staring at the viewscreen at the space beyond the ship's confines. Her shoulders slumped and a glass with what he assumed to be whiskey hung from one hand. Instead of turning, she lifted the glass and drained it. Then she straightened and squared her shoulders before turning.

"Admiral.".

Collins forced himself not to react. The Ashlyn Shaw standing before him bore a remarkable resemblance to the one he'd seen in a cell back on Fuercon mere days after she'd been brought back from the Tarsus penal colony. Her eyes were dead, her expression blank. She was an officer in pain, wishing she'd been on the shuttle with her people when they died.

While most of the taskforce's personnel looked forward to returning home, he saw the opposite in Ash. Returning home meant having to face not only her CO and the Commandant of the Marine Corps but also the families of the fallen. He knew she expected them to blame her for what happened. Worse, she accepted that blame. Somehow, he needed to push past that and get her to accept many more were coming home than would have if it weren't for her actions and those of her Marines.

"May we sit?" One corner of his mouth lifted in a smile as she started in surprise. Whatever she'd expected him to say, that hadn't been it. Good. If he could keep her off-balance, he had a chance to get through to her. He hoped.

"My apologies, Admiral." She looked around and then motioned to the sitting area. "May I get you a drink?"

"Thank you, no." He watched as she considered her now empty glass. When she placed it on the shelf next to the half-empty whiskey bottle, he blew out a soft sigh of relief. The second hurdle had been cleared.

"What can I do for you, sir?"

He leaned back did his best to look at ease as he waited for her to sit. "First off, you can relax. I wanted to talk to you about several things, including what's planned for tomorrow."

She nodded once.

"Ash, I'm not going to tell you to buck up or any of that bullshit." He chuckled as she leaned back, her eyes widening slightly in surprise. "Losing people sucks. That's the price of command and we both knew it when we accepted our commissions. But you've been hit with much more than that over the last five years and you haven't taken time— let's be honest, you haven't been given time—to come to terms with all that's happened. Now you've lost people you cared for due to yet another betrayal. That's enough to mess with anyone. So no, I'm not going to report you for it. All I'll do is say I'm here whenever you want to talk."

She swallowed hard and for a moment tears shone in her eyes before she blinked them back. "Thank you, sir."

"Richard," he corrected. "No formality tonight."

She nodded and gave a slight smile. "Thank you."

"You're due a little latitude, Ash." He relaxed a bit more. "We will assume a parking orbit around Fuercon tomorrow morning. Orders from FleetCom are to offload our dead first. I want full honor guards for each of your fallen. Mess Dress uniforms. Last off will be those who died in the shuttle saving this ship. With your permission, I would like to be one of the honor guard for them."

She nodded again. "Of course, sir, and thank you. Your taking part will mean a great deal to my people."

"Ash, I honor them as much as you do," he said gently. "And their deaths anger me just as much. That is one of the reasons why I will do everything I can to make sure Fonteneau and those who conspired with him feel the full wrath of our justice."

She didn't try to hide her emotions this time as she reached up and rubbed the tears from her eyes. "Thanks."

"After the fallen are handed over, you are to return to the ship." He held up a hand before she could protest. "I'll explain shortly. I think you'll approve."

"If you say so." She didn't sound convinced.

"Next off the ships will be the wounded. Then those who are being given leave or moving on to new assignments. Standard procedure in other words."

Ash reached for her datapad and made a few notes. "I'll make sure Marines are on-hand to assist in the bays."

"Thanks." He paused, considering what he needed to say next. "Once the port has been cleared of all but necessary personnel, the prisoners will be transported down. They will be taken into custody and secured in the brig in the security complex. I want you and a team you handpick to facilitate the transfer."

Ash blew out a breath and climbed to her feet. Collins waited, watching as she paced the length of the room. When she stopped in front of the viewscreen, he tensed slightly, wondering if she'd pour herself another drink. She'd been drinking too much since the loss of Talbot and the others. It hadn't impacted her performance—yet—but it was only a matter of time unless she stopped.

Damn it! Was asking her to deal with Fonteneau too much?

A moment later, Ash turned. As she did, she reached for the whiskey bottle. A rueful, almost sad, expression crossed her face. Then it was gone. Without a word, she moved across the room and put away the bottle. As she returned to her chair, Collins wondered if this was the turning point for her. He hoped so. If they were going to defeat the Callusians once and for all, they needed her sober and thinking, not dulling her senses and slowing her reflexes with liquor.

"I understand." She leaned forward, elbows on knees, chin resting on her upraised fists. When she leaned back a few moments later, she looked more like the Ashlyn Shaw he knew. Determination gleamed in her eyes and a hint of color touched her cheeks. "Richard—Admiral, I have one request."

He looked at her, a hint of suspicion starting to take root. "What?"

"I want to have a chat with Fonteneau." Now it was her turn to hold up a hand to keep him from interrupting. "Richard, I promise not to lay a hand on him. I won't even threaten him. But I have questions I need to ask. I owe it to the dead and to their families."

For several long moments, he considered what she said. Before he could answer, she smiled slightly and continued.

"I'm not asking you to let me see him alone. You can send anyone you want in with me. I even insist that the interview be recorded."

He didn't need to ask why. She'd learned the hard way to make sure she never left herself open to unfounded accusations if she could help it.

"All right, but with one proviso." He waited until she nodded for him to continue. "I will arrange it so you have a few minutes alone with him. I won't even tell you not to intimidate him. Just make sure you don't do or say anything that might negatively impact his trial."

"But?"

"You will do so after he's been handed off dirtside. Let's make this as clean as we can. Then you are to go home. Be with your son and the rest of your family until you have to report back for duty."

She smiled. It might have been a small smile, but it was the first real smile he'd seen from her since Talbot's death. "Thank you."

"One more thing." He climbed to his feet and waved for her to stay where she was. "Do you want me to assign someone to pack up Talbot's personal effects?"

"Thank you but no. My brother and I will do it tonight."

He reached out and rested a hand on her shoulder. He'd expected her answer and respected her for it.

"Briefing at 0700 to go over the final schedule for tomorrow. Get some rest now. There will be time to pack up Loco's belongings after the briefing."

With that, he turned and left her quarters. For the first time since Talbot's death, he felt better about Ashlyn and how she was coping. Hopefully, she was on the road to a return to normal.

# 4

---

AMBASSADOR D'ANIL Kalmár stared out the window, a frown pulling at the corners of his mouth. For five years he'd served as Midlothian's ambassador to Fuercon. Three of those had been before Derek Harper was elected as president. How he missed the days of the previous administration. Life had been much easier then.

Unlike his predecessor, Harper actually cared about his fellow Fuerconese, not just those who put him in power. He took his oaths to serve and protect them and the system seriously. Because of that, he didn't play political games, especially not if those games might put Fuercon at a disadvantage. That made Kalmár's job not only more difficult but decidedly more dangerous.

Damn Harper and damn Alexander Watchman!

Kalmár returned to his desk and once again pulled up the latest message from home. After weeks of delays, the government, in the form of the Administrative Bureau, finally responded to his request for guidance. Instead of giving him a clear policy to follow or, better yet, information on Watchman's location he could hand over to the Fuerconese, the Bureau played word games with him. He was to "appease" Harper. Give him whatever information he wanted, even if he had to make it up. All that really mattered was making sure he gave the man no reason to look closer at Midlothian than he was already. Then the Bureau reminded him he had a scapegoat—Watchman. All blame for any slights, real or imagined, presented by the Fuerconese were to be laid at the feet of the former Intelligence Czar.

Then came the threat. He'd been expecting it. One part of him was tempted to take them up on it. Midlothian's counterpart to Secretary of State Nelms reminded him he served at the pleasure of the Bureau. If he was unable to carry out these simple instructions, he left them with no recourse save to recall him home. There were dangers in going down that road but they couldn't be any worse than what he faced here, in a decidedly hostile environment.

If only it was that simple.

Kalmár ran a hand through his graying hair and dropped onto his chair. As he did, he released a long breath. Until he walked out of his office and seemingly disappeared into thin air, Alexander Watchman had been Midlothian's intelligence czar. He knew where all the bodies, real and metaphorical, were buried. He had dossiers on everyone in government and all the major business players. If the government wanted dirty work done, it turned to him and that gave him a power none of them anticipated. A power he never hesitated to use if he felt it would benefit him. Now those power players who never hesitated to use him to *deal with* those who became inconvenient or dangerous to them were scrambling to not only find him but to find his data stash before anyone else did. That included the Fuerconese and their allies.

The question remained about what Watchman planned. No one with an ounce of self-preservation believed he wouldn't reappear, probably at the worst possible moment. The real question wasn't when that happened but what Watchman would do when it did. Would he use the information he had on the members of the government as leverage in the face of the evidence Fuercon and her allies had gathered, evidence proving he had been working with the Callusians in the war?

Of course, he would. Kalmár didn't doubt it for a moment. Nor did he doubt Watchman would use the information to implicate those who failed to support him when their conspiracy became known.

Why in the name of all that was holy hadn't he retired when he had the chance before Harper took office? He wanted to be as far from here—and from Midlothian—as possible when the proverbial shit hit the fan.

A knock at the office door interrupted his thoughts. Sitting up, Kalmár called for the newcomer to enter. The door slid open and Elwyn Fertig stepped inside. The woman waited for the door to close. Then she activated the security screen that prevented anyone from entering or overhearing what was said. Worried, Kalmár waited, wondering what bad news the woman brought this time.

"Well?" he asked when she remained silent.

"I just received word that the taskforce sent to Savitar VI returned to the system last night. Shuttles have been arriving all morning, ferrying dead and injured groundside." She dropped onto one of the chairs in front of his desk. "I don't have any details, but word is Harper will address the system either tonight or tomorrow morning. My sources tell me the taskforce completed its mission but what it found was worse than anticipated. I'm trying to get additional details but, so far at least, no one is saying anything more than that."

Kalmár frowned again. Fertig was ostensibly his secretary. In reality, she had been sent by Watchman to keep an eye on him and on events on Fuercon. The ambassador knew first-hand how deadly she could be. Worse, he knew she would do whatever she felt necessary, even if it meant killing him, to protect Midlothian. But the woman sitting in front of him bore little resemblance to the confident killer he knew. This woman was shaken to her core and there could be only one explanation. She knew more than she said.

And he couldn't let that go unchallenged. Not when that knowledge could be about so many things that might mean life or death —for him.

"There's more to it. What aren't you telling me?"

Now it was her turn to frown. Kalmár held her gaze. Once he'd been scared of her and her ties to Watchman. But no more, at least that's what he told himself. She'd cut those ties when she handed Watchman's pet assassin over to the Fuerconese after Moreau attempted to assassinate President Harper. Oh, Fertig took a few precautions to make sure the woman couldn't give the Fuerconese any information about who she was or what she had been up to. But he knew what Watchman's orders had been. Fertig was to ensure Moreau's presence wasn't detected and, if it was, that she managed to get off-planet before she could be taken into custody.

Kalmár also knew Fertig never would have taken such a step had Watchman still been in power. But the revelation the Midlothians had actively assisted the Callusians in their war against Fuercon and her allies meant the government needed someone to blame. The last thing the system could afford was for her so-called allies to turn against it and declare war. Unlike Fuercon and the others, Midlothian didn't have a strong navy. It relied on money and trade to maintain its powerbase. That was now in danger because of Watchman and his belief he knew more and held more power than the government.

At least the powers-that-be had been quick to throw the blame on him. Not that it appeased Harper and his allies. They'd demanded Watchman be turned over to face judgement for his betrayal. But they also continued to dig and look for further evidence of a conspiracy. That led to others in the government and in the business sector being named as co-conspirators. Less than a month earlier, Harper had sent a final demand to the Midlothian government. Either hand over those named and all intel gathered about them and their whereabouts if they had fled the planet or the allies would take direct action against Midlothian.

Could that be why the taskforce returned home instead of remaining on-station?

"That's the problem." She lifted a hand and brushed the hair from her brow. "No one is saying anything else. My sources aren't talking. There is none of the usual chatter in the coffee shops and other stores near the port. Even my media contacts are getting the cold shoulder. I don't know if that means the taskforce got its ass kicked or if it found yet more evidence against Watchman or if it is something else."

Kalmár cursed softly. Harper had shut down most of their information sources before the taskforce left the system. Now it appeared he had finished the job. But why? And what did it portend for Midlothian in the long run?

"Keep on it. I don't care what you have to do, find out what's going on." He pinned her with a firm look. "And don't get caught at it."

Her eyes flashed and then she nodded.

"I'll see what I can find out from the diplomatic corps." Not that he expected it to be much. That source of information had dried up just as Fertig's sources had. "Any word on Watchman?"

She shook her head. "Nothing. He could be anywhere."

And that was what made him even more dangerous. They needed to find him and let the Fuerconese know before he managed to strike and cause even more trouble for Midlothian.

"Your recommendations?"

For a moment, she said nothing. Then she stood and paced the length of the office. He waited, giving her the chance to gather her thoughts. They might be uneasy allies now but at least they were allies. Not that he expected it to last. If Watchman turned up or if she felt it served her purposes to turn on him, she would without a second thought. Until then, however, Kalmár planned on using her. Hopefully, he'd have secured his position before she decided to try to do the same.

"We need to start preparing for having to move the staff and their dependents to the embassy. It won't take much more for the Fuerconese public to turn against us. Not with Harper telling them about Watchman working with the Callusian and his open speculation about what role the Bureau played in it all." She returned to her chair and sat. "I've been hearing reports of some of our people being verbally attacked when they've been out in public."

"I've already ordered preparations be made." He nodded toward the window overlooking Patriots Row, the roadway running in front of the embassy. "And our so-called protectors out there?"

He didn't have to explain who he meant. The uniformed members of the Fuerconese Marine Corps and capital security force patrolled outside the embassy. They might officially respect the sanctity of the embassy grounds, but he knew better. They were there as guards and would move in the moment Harper told them to.

"We continue to ignore them." She lifted a hand before he could say anything. "We can't do anything to give them cause to arrest our people or, worse, to make entry onto the embassy grounds. But we also have to be aware of the drones and the other forms of surveillance we must assume they are using."

He didn't like it but she was right. They had to play this smart and do their best to at least appear to be cooperating with the Fuerconese government.

"All right. Find me something I can use as leverage. A rumor about where Watchman might be, something about the Callusians, I don't care. We need to get Harper and his people off our backs until the home government has a plan in place to deal with this situation." He waited, giving her time to consider what he said. "And don't try to play me. Both our necks are on the line here."

"Believe me, I am well aware of that." She looked and sounded as if she appreciated the situation no more than he did.

"Any word on Moreau?"

This time Fertig cursed with such imagination he couldn't help smiling. Rarely did anything get under her skin, but the would-be assassin had. That was why he still didn't understand why Fertig left Moreau alive when she handed the woman over to the Fuerconese after that attack on Harper. The drug she gave Moreau might have locked down the woman's mind, preventing her from speaking or moving, but there was no guarantee the medical types wouldn't find a counteragent for it. If they did, Moreau could cost them everything.

"Nothing." She all but spat out the word. "The idiot medic I turned got himself reassigned to other patients. He won't say what happened but my guess is he did or said something to raise Shaw's suspicions. She's taken an interest in Moreau, from what he told me."

"The current medical team?"

She almost snarled before answering. "He doesn't know who is on it and I can't find out—yet. But I am working on it."

The possible implications worried him and, under cover of his desktop, Kalmár clinched one fist in anger. "All right. Keep trying. We need to know what's going on."

"What are you going to do?" she asked as she once again climbed to her feet.

"I think it might be time to meet again with Secretary Nelms. Perhaps reassuring him that we are acting in good faith and doing everything possible to locate Watchman and the others will help." Not that he expected it to.

Once alone, Kalmár reached for his comm. There was one call he needed to make before reaching out to Fuercon's secretary of state. This one might just keep him safe should Fertig decide to switch loyalties once again.

## 5

"COLONEL, I'M SORRY TO INTERRUPT BUT THERE'S A MILA TALBOT-Valois to see you."

Ashlyn set her reader to one side and looked up. Marie LeClerc, the family's long-time housekeeper, stood in the doorway to the study. She waited, her expression concerned, for Ash to reply. The problem was Ash didn't know what to say. She very badly wanted to tell the woman to inform their visitor that she wasn't home. But she couldn't—she wouldn't—do that, no matter how tempting it might be.

But how in the hell was she supposed to explain to Kevin Talbot's sister that he'd died because she'd failed to keep him safe?

Ash inhaled once, searching for the courage to face Talbot-Valois. "Show her in, Marie."

"Are you sure? I can tell her you are unavailable."

Ash smiled and shook her head. "It's all right, Marie. Show her in."

The woman gave Ash one last look before backing out of the room. As Marie closed the doors behind her, Ash smiled slightly. In the two days since her return home, Marie, as well as the rest of the family, had done their best to protect her. They knew she was hurting. Because of that, they'd run interference, keeping the media at bay. They went with her to the funerals of some of those who fell during the mission to Savitar VI. There were more funerals to come, including the memorial service for Talbot, and she had no doubt they would be there as well.

God, how was she going to get through Talbot's memorial service?

Ash stood and moved across the study to stand in front of the windows making up the far wall. That was her command instinct taking control. It put her in the position of power, not that she felt powerful just then. All she felt was a numbing grief and guilt. But she hadn't had more than a glass of wine at dinner since her return. She knew better than to risk losing control around her family. They would understand but her mother would be honor bound to report it to General Okafor and the last thing Ash wanted was to be grounded. She needed to be out there, fighting the enemy and making them pay for each and every death suffered on this mission and all the others.

"Ms. Talbot-Valois, Colonel," Marie said from the doorway a few minutes later.

Ash turned away from the window and her breath caught. Mila Talbot-Valois stood just as tall and confident as her brother had. They shared the same facial structure and her eyes were the same color as his had been. But it was the grief and something else reflected in those dark eyes that stopped Ashlyn's breath for a moment. Then she steeled herself, prepared for the verbal barrage she knew to be coming.

"Thank you for seeing me, Colonel Shaw. I won't take much of your time," Talbot-Valois said as Marie closed the doors behind her.

"Please have a seat." Ash indicated the sofa against the wall to her right. She waited for the woman to sit before taking one of the chairs opposite a low coffee table in front of it. "Is there anything the regiment can do for you or your family?"

She'd see to it they did everything possible to help. Unfortunately, they couldn't do the one thing they all wanted. They couldn't bring Talbot or any of the others back to life.

"No but thank you. I promise we will let you know if we need anything." Talbot-Valois shifted almost nervously on the sofa.

"Colonel, I won't take long. But I wanted to thank you for myself and for my family."

Ash's brows knit and she looked at the woman in confusion. Thank her? For what?

"I don't understand."

Talbot-Valois smiled almost gently. Then she stood and moved to sit in the chair next to Ashlyn's. "May I call you Ashlyn?"

Ash nodded, not trusting herself to speak.

"Ashlyn, you may not remember, but we've met before. It wasn't long after your first assignment on the *Heinlein*."

A slight smile touched Ash's lips as she remembered the time. The *Heinlein* had returned to Fuercon a month earlier. Soon Ash would be shipping out again, this time on the *Ascendant*. One night a week or so before she was due to report to her new posting, she'd met with some of her former shipmates for dinner and drinks. Talbot had been there. He'd brought his younger sister who was home from university for a few days. Mila Talbot sat quietly most of the night, watching her brother with undisguised admiration. Then, not long before Ash left, the young woman asked if they could talk. Ash had nodded and they'd excused themselves before stepping outside, away from the noise of the crowded tavern.

Talbot's sister had wanted to thank her then as she apparently did now. Back then, it was for being her big brother's friend. Ash assured her it was her pleasure and told her how the man had been friend and mentor to her. Then she'd made the younger woman promise to let her know if she ever needed anything. That was the one and only time she'd seen Mila. Now that shy young woman barely out of her teens was the sophisticated and confident professional who was once again thanking her.

"I remember. I told you then to let me know if you ever needed anything." She managed a slight smile, knowing it didn't reach her eyes.

"And you gave me the one thing I wanted." Talbot-Valois reached for her hand. "You gave my brother your friendship and respect. You gave him the confidence he needed to become the Marine he was. Now I have something to give you. Something I hope you will accept."

Ash looked at her in question.

"Ashlyn, do you know what I do as a profession?"

For a moment, Ash considered the question. Then she nodded once, remembering a conversation she and Talbot had not long after her pardon. "Kevin told me. He was so very proud of you when you passed your boards. The fact you chose to work with active duty military and our vets meant the world to him."

Tears gathered in the woman's eyes and she blinked them back. "He's a large reason why I went into the profession. I saw what some of the missions did to him emotionally You Marines, especially the Devil Dogs, are on the front lines. You see the death and destruction of war up close. You live with the reality that you may not return from your next mission. You've seen your friends, your brothers and sisters, die or worse. It takes a toll and I wanted to do what I could to help people like you and my brother deal with it before it broke you."

Ash glanced at the woman's hand resting on hers. When she looked up, tears burned in her eyes. "I would do anything to turn the clock back. You have to know that."

"I do." She gave Ashlyn's hand a squeeze and then leaned back. "Ashlyn, you need to forgive yourself. You aren't to blame for what happened to my brother and the others. The only ones who are or either dead or you transported them back here to face justice."

Ash blinked in surprise. That information was supposed to be classified. How had she found out?

Talbot-Valois smiled almost gently. "Don't look so suspicious. General Okafor told me when she met with the family yesterday."

Ash inhaled deeply. Had the general also asked the woman to come here and evaluate her?

"Don't look so worried." Once again, Talbot-Valois leaned over and patted her hand. "I'm here simply because I feel like I know you from everything Kevin said over the years. Because of that, and because of what you meant to my brother, I wanted to make sure you knew we didn't blame you for what happened."

Ash considered getting to her feet and moving across the room. This interview was going nothing like she anticipated. She didn't know whether to let it play out or to run for the hills. That had her glancing around the room. One corner of her mouth twitched as she realized the doors weren't completely closed. Marie had left them open a crack and she had no doubt the woman waited on the other side, ready to intervene if necessary.

"At the risk of repeating myself, I don't understand."

"My brother meant the world to me, Ashlyn. I won't lie. There have been times when I've been jealous of the Corps and the way he loved it and many of his fellow Marines. He thought of the Devil Dogs like family. Some he was closer to than others, as it is with any family. But you, Colonel Ortega, Sgt. Major Anisimova and a few others were like brothers and sisters to him."

The woman chuckled softly, almost as if to herself. "He often said you and Anisimova made him into the man and the Marine he was. Anisimova because she wouldn't let him slack and pushed him to be the best he could. You because you showed him there really are offi-cers, even wet behind the ears butterbars, who give a damn about their troops and who will do everything possible to bring them all home alive."

"He's the one who made me a better Marine." Ash spoke softly, her gaze resting on her hands in her lap.

"Let's compromise and say you made each other better." Talbot-Valois waited until she agreed. "I remember how he reacted when you and the others were first arrested and charged after the Arterus mission. It was all we could do to keep him from storming the secu-rity complex to try to break you out. Of course, he wasn't the only one considering doing just that. I think that's the first time I realized how much of an impression you made on not only my brother but others in the Corps.

"I'm not breaking confidence when I say I counseled a number of those same Marines after your conviction. I came out of those sessions with a better picture of you and why your Marines are so willing to follow you to Hell and back." She turned in her chair a little so she could fully look Ash in the eyes. "You care. You never ask them to do anything you wouldn't do yourself. You have, on more than one occasion, stood between them and some other officer who was willing to send them to their deaths without cause. You would rather die than have one of them lose their lives." She paused and smiled gently as Ash reached up to brush away a stray tear that rolled down her cheek.

"Now I want you to understand something. Your Marines, people like my brother, felt the same way about you. They would gladly put themselves between the enemy and you because they know how important you are to the war effort. I know my brother well enough to realize he never hesitated when he made the decision to use the shuttle to intercept the missile heading toward the flagship. I also have no doubt the others onboard agreed completely and without hesitation with the plan.

"And I know you blame yourself for their deaths because you couldn't change their minds before the missile struck the shuttle. It is worse for you because you saw what happened. You spoke with Kevin moments before the moment the shuttle intercepted the missile. It was probably the only time he refused a direct order from you and you feel guilty he and the others sacrificed themselves as they did."

Ash nodded, emotion closing her throat and preventing her from speaking.

"You need to remember something, Ashlyn. The last thing any of those brave men and women would want is for you to feel responsible for what happened. You have nothing to feel guilty about. Hell, Colonel, if they knew how you were feeling, they'd probably come back from the dead to beat some sense into you. Accept the fact they did exactly what you would have done had your roles been reversed."

Ash closed her eyes. She didn't want to admit it but Talbot-Valois was right. Any one of those Marines on the shuttle would have been the first to volunteer for a suicide mission on the ground. Their sense of duty and willingness to do whatever it took to protect Fuercon and its allies was why they'd been Devil Dogs.

God, it wasn't fair they were gone and she was still there.

"It's called survivor's guilt, Ash. You've felt it before. It's common for those in battlefield situations to feel it. But you've been dealt one blow after another over the last few years: the Arterus mission, your court martial and conviction, the time in the penal colony, your return home only to be thrown immediately into the middle of a new war, Colonel Pawlak's death and then Colonel Ortega's. I doubt you've given yourself time, much less permission, to grieve and now you suffer the loss of my brother and the others. Please, let yourself be human. Let your grief out. Don't let it, don't let the enemy, beat you."

She knew Talbot-Valois was right. But it was hard, so very hard, to accept it. She should have known what Talbot and the others planned. After all, it's exactly what she would have done had she been in their place. Now she had to find her way through it. She'd never forget them. She never forgot any of her dead.

"How do you do it?" she asked softly.

"I grieve. That's a necessary part of the process. But I don't carry their deaths with me like you do."

"I guess I've been an idiot, haven't I?"

"Not at all. You've been too hard on yourself but it is understandable. It's easier to do that than it is to admit you could have done nothing. None of us like being helpless."

That was certainly the truth.

"Thank you." This time Ash reached over and grasped the woman's hand.

Talbot-Valois smiled and patted her hand. "I do have a favor to ask. Two actually."

"Anything."

"My family has finalized the arrangements for Kevin's memorial service. Would you do us the honor of not only choosing his honor guard and pall bearers but of being one as well?"

Ash swallowed hard and nodded. "It would be my honor."

Her guest smiled. "There's one more thing." Now she reached into her jacket pocket. Ash watched as she pulled out a chain. Hanging from it was a dog tag. Ash's breath caught and her heart pounded as she guessed what it was. "Before he shipped out his very first time, Kevin had extra dog tags made for the family. He knew even then the possibility that he might die and his body not be recovered. He wanted us to have these to remember him by."

"Most of us do that," Ash said softly.

"Much as Kevin loved you, he adored your son. After your court martial, my brother rewrote his will. He left Jake a bequest that should help with his education costs later. At the same time, he asked me to give one of his tags to your son if anything ever happened to him. Is that all right?"

Ash pressed the heels of her hands to her eyes. Emotion tightened her chest. Kevin Talbot had never forgotten the promise he made to her before her trial. He swore he'd make sure her son was safe. Back then, she'd worried about the little boy's biological father taking him and preventing her family from being a part of Jake's life. She'd known Talbot and others from the Devil Dogs would do whatever it took to make sure her son was all right. Thank God, her ex had screwed up quickly and her parents took custody of Jake.

"Your brother was a truly special man," she whispered as she stood. A moment later, she opened the door and asked Marie to bring Jake to the study. "Are you sure about this?" she asked as she returned to her chair.

"I am." Talbot-Valois smiled and even though her sadness at the loss of her brother was there to see so was her determination to carry through his final wishes.

A few minutes later, Jake slipped into the room. Seeing his mother, he ran to her. Ash dropped to one knee and pulled him close. For a moment, she held him close, wondering how she was going to get through the next few minutes. Then she shook herself. Her son had loved Talbot as much as the man had loved him. Jake would mourn his loss but he would also do whatever he could to make the man proud of him.

"Jake, I want you to meet someone." She stood and took his hand in hers before leading him to stand before Talbot-Valois. "This is Dr. Mila. She's Uncle Kevin's sister."

"I'm pleased to meet you," the boy said and freed his hand from his mother's grasp before extending it to Talbot-Valois. "I'm sorry about Uncle Kevin. I miss him."

"Me too, Jake." The woman slipped to her knees in front of him, putting them at the same eye level. "Long ago, when you were just a little boy, my brother asked me to do something for him if anything ever happened. Do you know what it was?"

Jake looked at his mother before shaking his head.

"He wanted me to give you this." She extended her right hand, the dog tag and chain resting on her palm.

"Jake, that is one of Uncle Kevin's dog tags. Dr. Mila and her family would like it very much if you'd wear it in honor of Uncle Kevin," Ash explained.

He reached out and gently touched the tag. "Mama, like you wear Aunt Lucinda's?"

"That's right, Jake. Just like I wear Aunt Lucinda's." And her grandfather's and many times removed great grandmother's.

"I'd like that."

Talbot-Valois leaned forward and gently kissed his cheek. Then she draped the chain over his head and closed his hand over the single dog tag. "You do my family a great honor, Jake." She reached up with her left hand and brushed away a tear.

"We're your family now, Dr. Mila," the little boy said.

Pride filled Ash. "He's right, Mila. You are family. Not just where the Devil Dogs are concerned but where my family is as well. I hope you remember that."

"Thank you." Talbot-Valois climbed to her feet and then bent to give Jake a hug.

"Run on, son. Ask Marie to fix you a snack. I'll join you in a few minutes," Ash told him and watched as he left the room, his hand still wrapped around the dog tag. "Thank you."

"I should be the one thanking you, Ashlyn." She surprised Ash by giving her a quick hug. "I'll email the details of the memorial service to you. After it's over, would you and your family join us for a meal? It would mean the world to my parents to get to talk to you about Kevin."

Ash nodded. It would be hard, but Talbot-Valois was right. She needed to forgive herself and let herself grieve. Perhaps this was the first step in doing so.

"We'd love to, Mila." She walked to the study door with the woman. "I'll talk to you later tonight about the honor guard and pall bearers."

Talbot-Valois turned to face her. As she did, she rested a hand on Ashlyn's arm. "We both loved him and we both mourn him. Now let's find a way to avenge him and all the others who died."

That was one thing Ash was more than happy to promise to do.

6

---

THE MORNING AFTER TALBOT'S MEMORIAL SERVICE, GENERAL HELEN Okafor leaned back as she finished reviewing Rico Santiago's latest intel report. The colonel and his people had worked around the clock since Taskforce Liberator's return. Part of Santiago's team slowly combed through all the data the taskforce brought back. Others interviewed the prisoners. As if that wasn't enough, the investigation into Evan Moreau continued. Not in recent memory had the various intelligence services worked so many different threads that all seemed to lead to the same source: the Callusians. The pressing questions needing immediate answers were question was how much the Midlothians had known, especially about the events in Savitar VI and the biotoxin used there, and how much intel about Fuercon and her allies had they turned over to the Callusians.

Now she faced another possible dilemma, one she had put off dealing with long enough.

"General, they're here," her aide announced over the comm.

"Ask Sgt. Major Anisimova to join us. Then send them in," Okafor said.

"Brigadier General Shaw and Colonel Shaw, ma'am," the aide said a few moments later. "The sergeant major is on her way."

"Thank you. Send in coffee for everyone and then make sure we aren't disturbed."

With that, the Commandant of the Marine Corps stood and moved around her desk. As she did, the newcomers braced to attention. She held them there for a moment, her eyes missing no detail of their appearance. Other than a faint hint of concern in Elizabeth's eyes, the woman looked as she always did: competent and ready for action.

Ashlyn, however, was a different matter. She looked drawn. Dark shadows bruised the skin under her eyes and Okafor wondered if she'd gotten much sleep since returning home. Grief etched lines from the bridge of her nose to the corners of her mouth. It would take time for the grief to ease. Fortunately, the guilt Okafor had seen the few times she and Ash crossed paths since Taskforce Liberator's return appeared to have lessened. Good. Hopefully, Ash was finally coming to terms with what happened. That too, the general knew, would take time.

Unfortunately, unless something changed, they didn't have much time and she needed Ashlyn back to normal sooner rather than later.

"Have a seat," she said as the door slid open once again.

Sergeant Major of the Marine Corps Edita Anisimova stepped inside. She carried a tray with several carafes and four mugs. As the door shut behind her, she crossed the office and placed the tray on the edge of Okafor's desk. As she poured for everyone, she arched one blonde brow in Okafor's direction.

"Before we get started, I want to say something." Okafor noted how both of the Shaws stiffened. Elizabeth cast a quick glance at her daughter before once again turning her attention to the general. "I have no doubt you've both already told the families of the fallen to let you know if they need anything. I want to know as well. The Corps will stand by them, no matter what."

Ash swallowed and her lips thinned into a hard line before she nodded. "I will, ma'am. So far, they seem to be all right."

Okafor nodded once. "Liz, I want you to push though the paperwork getting them death benefits and any other payouts they are due."

"My staff is already on it, ma'am," Elizabeth said.

"Thank you. I knew I could count on you." She leaned back and sipped her coffee. As she did, she waved for Anisimova to quit hovering and to take a seat.

"I've had a chance to review your end of mission reports, Ash. I know you aren't ready to hear this but I'm going to say it anyway. You and your people did everything possible and it is because of that dedication and hard work we didn't lose more people. None of us could have anticipated the betrayal by Fonteneau."

"Thank you, ma'am." Ash glanced down at her mug and then looked up, meeting Okafor's gaze. "Ma'am, this may be my paranoia speaking, but we need to start considering the possibility of betrayal on a wider scale. This is the second time now our military has been put at a distinct disadvantage by someone we assumed to be an ally."

"Trust me, Ash, it is something the powers that be are well aware of. Even as we speak, President Harper, SecDef and others are discussing the best way to proceed." For a moment, Okafor considered if she should say anything more. "The three of you, and especially you, Ash, need to know I have made my concerns very clear not only to FleetCom but to SecDef and President Harper. My oaths as Commandant of the Corps aren't limited to protecting Fuercon and its interests. They extend to doing everything I can to maintain the strength of the Corps. That includes making sure we aren't at risk of having our forces wiped out due to betrayal."

"I'm glad this is now something being considered." Elizabeth glanced again at her daughter and it was easy to guess what she was thinking. It could just as easily have been Ashlyn's shuttle that had been destroyed as Talbot's.

"You worked closely with the medicals on the mission to find a protocol that would keep your people safe and still not put the rest of the taskforce in danger when the Marines returned from Shennong's surface, Ash. Your reports and theirs have been forwarded to the medical division and the bio-research department. The armorers have been read in. Each of those departments will be reaching out to you to go over your reports. I want you to collaborate with them to see if there is any way to improve on what you and the others came up with.

"Our goal right now is multi-pronged. The first is to do everything possible to ensure our armor can protect our Marines should they be caught groundside when the biotoxin is released again. And we are operating on the assumption Shennong was not a once and done situation. This is exactly the sort of weapon the Callusians can and will use against a major population area in an attempt to intimidate the rest of the allies into surrender. We can't allow that to happen."

"I'll do everything I can to help, General."

"Of more concern is what protocols should be put into place onboard our ships. The samples taken from the post-battle debris show the biotoxin had been loaded into at least several one of the torpedoes. There is good reason to believe there was more of it still onboard the enemy flagship. I don't need to tell you what could happen if one of those warheads penetrated a ship's hull."

Ash blanched slightly and nodded.

"We can't be in full armor all the time, General."

From Anisimova's tone, Okafor had a pretty good idea she would like nothing more. At least until they had a cure for the biotoxin.

"Admiral Tremayne has recommended ships maintain battle station readiness, at least with regard to compartment hatches. Admiral Collins agreed with the recommendation and that means FleetCom is taking it seriously. As Admiral Tremayne noted, it will make moving through the ship more inconvenient, but it will hopefully contain the spread of the biotoxin should it be introduced to a ship."

"What about ventilation systems?" Ash asked, placing her mug on the floor at her feet.

"FleetCom is still working on the best way to handle that complication. My guess is that by the end of the week, new protocols, both for while in battle and for when approaching a new system, will be ready for presentation to FleetCom. This is where you, Liz and Edita come into play. I want the three of you to work together to formulate new protocols for our front-line Marines."

"Are we to assume the new protocols have been put into place or not?" Elizabeth asked.

"Both. It will take time to get the word out and to get armor updated. So walk them through the safety measures you took, Ash, and the whys of it. Add the new protocol after that."

"Understood, ma'am."

"Once that's done, we'll be meeting with Admiral Collins and his team to compare notes and refine everything before presenting it to FleetCom."

Okafor lifted her mug and frowned to find it empty. Almost instantly, Anisimova was there to refill it before offering to refill everyone else's mugs.

"Liz, Ash, you need to know one more thing. The elements of the division not already moving into place for the push to the Callusian home system will remain in-system until the new protocols are finalized and we are sure the home system is protected. That means the Navy will be moving some of its elements around. I will also be moving some of our elements around to make sure we have enough ships and bodies in place to repel the Callusians if they decide to come after Fuercon with the biotoxin."

"General," Ashlyn all but growled. "The longer we wait, the longer they have to recover from losing Dadd and his ships. Hell, it means they have longer to deploy the biotoxin at a new target."

"That is unfortunate but it is necessary."

"The hell it is!" Ash exploded out of her chair.

Okafor shook her head quickly, stopping both Elizabeth and Anisimova from responding. Instead, she leaned back and watched as Ash stalked across the office. She'd expected the reaction and, in a way, was glad to see it. The younger woman had been holding her emotions under too tight of control since before Lucinda Ortega's death. She would rather have Ash lose control here, among those who cared for her and who could talk her down, than to have it happen in the middle of battle where it could get her and others killed.

"General, we have the advantage," Ashlyn said as she turned to face them. "The fact they haven't used the biotoxin against another target seems to confirm our suspicion that they are not yet producing it in large quantities. We can't afford to wait until they can do so. Nor can we afford to wait for someone to step into Dadd's shoes, someone who may be even more ruthless and unpredictable than he was."

"And we can't afford to send ships and personnel into battle without making sure they are prepared to deal with the biotoxin."

Ashlyn's hands fisted at her side.

"General, you weren't there. You didn't see an entire planet wiped out by a biological. No life other than vegetation survived. The biotoxin acts quickly, usually within less than an hour. It is an agonizing death. We can't wait. If we do and they hit another planet, those deaths will be on us. Can you live with that? Because I sure as hell can't."

"Colonel, would you rather have more dead Marines on our hands?"

"General!" Elizabeth snapped as Ashlyn went as still as stone.

"General Okafor, if you have to ask that, then it is time for me to resign my commission." Ashlyn spoke slowly, almost robotically. As she did, she reached into the thigh pocket of her trousers and pulled out her ID. She glanced briefly at it before tossing it onto Okafor's desk.

"Everyone, shut up and take a breath!" Anisimova ordered. She leaned over and grabbed up the ID and carried it back to Ashlyn. As she shoved it into the younger woman's hand, she jabbed a finger in the direction of the chair Ash occupied earlier. "Sit down and don't say a word, not a fucking word – ma'am."

Okafor fought the urge to smile. She knew she'd taken a risk by pushing Ash. A risk not just with Ashlyn but with Elizbeth as well. Both were on edge and for good reason. But she needed them thinking and not just reacting. She only hoped she hadn't gone too far.

"Now, before you do something exceptionally stupid and that would force me to kick your ass, Colonel, you are going to sit there and listen to what the general has to say. Trust me, if she doesn't explain pretty damned quickly, it may be her ass I'm kicking."

The look the sergeant major sent her had Okafor fighting to hold back her laugh.

"And you are going to remember that each of us knows we may give up our lives in the defense of Fuercon and her allies whenever we leave home. That's what we signed up for when we joined the Corps. Honor your dead by remembering what they fought for and why they did so. Don't you dare blame yourself for what happened. If you do, I swear I will find a way to resurrect Talbot just so he can join me in kicking your ass—ma'am."

"Be careful, Durga, or I'll find a way to poach you from this cushy assignment." Ashlyn's threat rang hollow even as her eyes danced with laughter.

"I dare you to, ma'am."

"And I will bust all three of you down to private if you try," Okafor countered. This was not going the way she expected. Even so, it was a relief to see Ashlyn letting go of her anger, at least for the moment.

"As for your concerns, Ash, I assure you we aren't just sitting here waiting to see what the Callusians do next. Our forward elements are continuing with their mission. There has been one change to their orders, however. They are to harass any Callusian elements they come across. The point is to keep focus on them as they lead the Callusians away from the enemy home system. We have to keep them from taking too close of a look at what we are doing. It will also, hopefully, give our allies time to strengthen their own defenses because when we make the final push, we will be pulling much of our support from all the allied systems. President Harper wants to end this war once and for all.

"But we have to be smart about it. That is why we're taking the steps I laid out. If you have a problem with it, you either learn to live with it or I will transfer you to another division. Don't doubt that for one moment. I don't want to, and it would weaken our forces if I do. But I can't have a loose cannon running the 10$^{th}$. So decide here and now whether you are going to follow orders or move on."

She pinned Ashlyn with a firm look that all but dared the younger woman to say anything except "yes, ma'am."

Ash held Okafor's gaze for a moment, then she dropped her head into her hands. Silence filled the room as they waited, giving her the time she needed. Elizabeth reached over and gently rubbed her daughter's back. Anisimova stood between Okafor's desk and the two women, her expression still thunderous. Okafor had a feeling her sergeant major would have more than a few choice words once they were alone.

Not that she didn't deserve them.

When Ashlyn looked up, Okafor waited. Had the woman finally broken? She wouldn't blame Ash if she had. No one could go through everything she had the last few years without being scarred both physically and emotionally. The question was if those scars were so deep she couldn't come back from them.

Without a word, Ash stood and braced to attention. She remained that way until Okafor nodded, giving her permission to speak. The general's pulse quickened as she wondered what the younger woman wanted to say.

"General Okafor, General Shaw, Sgt. Major Anisimova, my apologies for my behavior. There are no excuses. I was insubordinate and disrespectful. I did not live up to the standard I demand of those under my command. If you feel discipline is required, I won't object."

Okafor sighed and then hid her grin behind her hand as Anisimova rolled her eyes. Knowing the sergeant major as well as she did, she decided to let her speak first. With a dip of her chin, she leaned back and watched as Anisimova moved to stand in front of Ashlyn. As she did, Elizabeth stood, her expression wary.

"Colonel Shaw, are you trying to force me to kick your ass?"

Anisimova's tone was conversational and Okafor chuckled softly. She'd seen the woman use that same tone too many times before ripping some poor private, or junior officer, a new one. From the way Ashlyn's eyes widened slightly before she had her expression under control again, Okafor guessed she knew what the woman was up to as well.

"Negative, Sgt. Major." Ashlyn continued to look forward, her eyes focused on some point above Okafor's head.

"Then would you explain why you are showing even less common sense than a certain butter bar did when I first met her?"

Now Elizabeth chuckled and relaxed as she returned to her seat.

"I believe that butter bar would be doing the same thing I am now, Sgt. Major." Ash cut her eyes to where Anisimova stood before once again looking straight ahead. "And the senior officer that butter bar became knows she fucked up. Pardon the language, General Okafor."

"The language is appropriate to the situation, Colonel." Okafor stood and strode around her desk to stand next to Anisimova. "I have one question for you, Colonel. Do you want to help defeat the Callusians once and for all and make sure that what happened to you and your people, to the citizens of Shennong happens to no one else?"

"That's two questions, ma'am." Ashlyn's lips twitched as she fought her smile. "But the answer is yes."

"Then stand easy and relax." She waited until Ashlyn did as she ordered. Then she reached out and rested a hand on the younger woman's arm. "Ash, you have to forgive yourself for what happened to Talbot. I know you mourn the deaths of all those under your command, especially those on the shuttle. But I also know it is Talbot's death that haunts you. Each of us have been there. We understand what you are feeling and we know what it takes to move on. Talk to us. Let us help you. The Corps needs you at your best right now and Talbot wouldn't thank you for retreating into guilt or into a bottle."

Ashlyn swallowed hard before nodding once.

"I want you and the good sergeant major here to put your heads together now. Pull together some exercises to keep your people busy. They need to work through their own anger and grief. Then get started on new protocols. Captain Adamson and Lieutenant Connery can oversee the regiment today."

"Yes, ma'am."

"Dismissed."

She watched as the two left her office. As the door shut behind them, she blew out a long breath and dropped onto the chair next to Elizabeth.

"That was too close, Helen," the woman said.

"I know, but it was necessary." Even if Ashlyn never forgave her.

"Remember that when my daughter decides to make good on her threat to poach Anisimova from you."

She threw her head back and laughed before sobering. "She'd better not try."

Elizabeth simply smiled and Okafor knew she'd been played. Well, she deserved it. But that didn't mean she wouldn't get payback. The only question was when.

---

ASH FOLLOWED Anisimova to the sergeant major's office. It didn't surprise her when the blonde not only closed the door behind them but initiated security protocols so they wouldn't be interrupted. What did surprise her was seeing the woman produce a bottle of whiskey from her bottom desk drawer.

"Are you ready to talk about it now?" Anisimova quickly poured out drinks for the two of them and handed Ash a glass.

Ash lifted one shoulder in a shrug and slumped back in her chair. "How badly did I fuck up with the general?"

"You didn't."

Ashlyn's eyebrows winged up in surprise and Anisimova chuckled softly.

"Kid, she pushed you and she did so on purpose. She's been worried about you. We all have. We know how much Loco meant to you. His death, coming so close to Lucinda's, was going to impact you negatively. As the commandant, Okafor needed to know how badly. More than that, she needed to know if you could bounce back."

"So she played me." Ash didn't know if she approved or not.

"She did." The blonde took a sip of her whiskey eased a hip onto the corner of her desk. "Now answer my question. Are you ready to talk about it?"

Ash swirled her whiskey, watching the light refracting through it. Then she tossed it back, shaking her head when Anisimova offered her a refill. She'd drunk more in the time since Talbot's death than she had in years. It was time to stop. Maybe talking with Anisimova, someone who knew the man and cared for him as much as she did, would help.

It sure as hell couldn't hurt.

"You've seen the videos of what happened on Shennong."

Anisimova nodded, her expression grim.

"Trust me, it was much worse in person. Some of those infected died within minutes of being exposed to the biotoxin. Others took longer. Those tried to get home or to find help. They died in agony." Ash closed her eyes and the images she'd seen while dirtside returned as real as if she was once again standing on Shennong.

"Durga, it wasn't just the people. Birds fell from the sky. Animals died where they stood. The only things left alive were vegetation and insect. It was eerie and reminded me of some of my worst nightmares as a kid." She stood and placed her glass on the woman's desk. As she crossed to the far side of the office, she shuddered.

"The only thing we heard when we left the shuttles was the sound of the wind and the occasional buzzing of an insect. It was eerie and we didn't know if the precautions we'd taken would be enough to save ourselves, much less the taskforce.

"When Collins ordered me back to the ship, I knew the shit was about to hit the fan. We'd been expecting the Callusians to return. Nothing about their attack on the system felt right. Why use the biotoxin on Shennong instead of the capital planet or one of the more populated planets in the system? Then there was the question about why the Callusians ships left the system before our arrival. We'd seen enough of the system government by then to know it would have surrendered had it been given the option."

"That's why Collins set up the additional defense platforms and didn't tell Fonteneau about them."

Ash nodded. "Neither of us trusted Fonteneau but we didn't have anything other than our suspicions to go on. So we read our senior officers and NCOs in on the situation and did our best to anticipate anything that might happen. But we fucked up. We didn't think that bastard would try to deactivate the defense platforms with our ships in-system."

She rubbed a hand over her face and drew in a shaky breath. "My shuttle made it back to the flagship before the attack began. But the decon process took several hours to complete. The other shuttles were held dirtside because we needed to get our people back to the DZ. Then they had to go through the initial decon process there before returning to the ships.

"Loco and the others made the decision, and Collins and I approved it, to return to the taskforce once they cleared decon. The other shuttles would return as soon as they could. By then, the battle had begun. We knew it was dangerous for the shuttle, but we were in the fight of our lives and every able body was needed."

She paused, forcing herself not to relive the battle. She'd done so too many times, awake and sleeping, already.

"Both Collins and I tried waving the shuttle off. The fighting was intense and Collins had authorized what was basically our last-ditch effort to stop the enemy. We'd lost a couple of ships already. The others, including ours, were damaged. Our shields were failing. Just as we targeted their flagship, they targeted ours.

"You know what those moments are like. You don't know if your shields will hold or if the countermeasures will work. You're praying as hard as you can even as you're doing everything possible to keep your people alive. It was at that point our countermeasures failed to take out all the enemy torpedoes."

Fear returned with the memory of those last few minutes of the battle. A bead of sweat ran down her spine. For what seemed an eternity, her memories held her. Then she shook them off.

"That's when we realized the shuttle was moving into position. We raised them and tried to wave them off. Loco." She stopped and swallowed hard as emotion tried to close her throat. "Loco said they knew what they were doing. Each of them had talked about it and agreed this was their only course of action. H-he said it had been an honor to serve with me. There was a bit more and then they were gone. They intercepted the missile that would have struck the ship."

Tears ran down her cheeks. "If they'd followed orders, they would have lived. They didn't have to play the hero."

She scrubbed away her tears. Then she was in Anisimova's arms. Together they mourned for each of those on the shuttle but most especially for the man who had been friend and brother by choice.

"He made the same choice you would have. The same choice I would have, Ash." Anisimova led her to a chair and waited as she was seated. Then she sat next to her. "You know that, just as you know he'd kick your ass for letting his death knock you for a loop like it has."

Ash nodded. She knew it but that didn't make the loss any less.

"Look at me, kid."

Ashlyn did as she said.

"You're always going to miss him. Just as you'll miss Lucinda. They were more than fellow Marines. They were your closest friends and you knew they were two you could always count on."

Ash nodded.

"Don't try to ignore your feelings. Experience them and move on. Holding it all in will only hurt you and it does a disservice to them." She reached out and rested her hand on one of Ashlyn's. "But you need to do more. You celebrate their memories. You teach those coming up the ranks about them and keep their memory alive in the Corps. You remind Jake about his Uncle Kevin and Aunt Lucinda and how much they loved him. And you take the fight to the enemy once we are in position to do so. Make them pay for the deaths of our friends and for the deaths of every Marine under your command."

Ash closed her eyes and nodded. Anisimova was right. It was time to focus on the future, not regret the events of the past. If only doing so was as easy as recognizing the need.

"That means finding a replacement for Loco." Something she wasn't ready to do yet.

"And Okafor isn't going to force you to do so – yet. There's plenty of other things you need to do first. And, when you're ready to start considering candidates, I'm here to help."

"Thanks." She grinned then. "We could tell the general you're joining my staff."

Anisimova laughed and shook her head. "Don't tempt me. The hardest thing I've ever done as a Marine is remain safe on Fuercon while I watch the rest of you take the fight to the enemy."

"I can imagine. But you need to know how much we appreciate knowing someone who understands what it means to be on the front lines is sitting where you do. You and Okafor know what it means to be a Marine. More than that, you know what it means to be a Devil Dog. That's a hell of a lot more than we had under the previous administration."

Which was putting it mildly.

"I hope so." Anisimova smiled and leaned back in her chair. "There's one thing the general didn't tell you. Other than when you are meeting with your mother and me about the new protocols, you are on leave for the rest of the week. The same order has gone out to the others in the regiment who were on the mission with you. Spend the time with Jake. Recharge and give yourself time to recover. You'll be busy enough next week when you return to duty."

"Why don't you join us this weekend?" Ash suggested. "No work. I promise. But it will help Jake to see you."

"I think it will help me to see him." Her expression softened and a small smile touched her lips. "He was so grown up at Kevin's funeral. It about did me in seeing him marching next to you as you and the others carried in the casket."

"I didn't know he planned to do that." And it had made her extremely proud. "He told me later that he's going to be a gunny just like Uncle Kevin." She grinned as Anisimova threw her head back and laughed.

"That must chap your mother's ass." The blonde laughed again. "Her family is thick with outstanding officers, present company included. To hear her grandson wants to be a lowly gunny." She chuckled almost evilly.

"Oh, I think we can cure him of that ambition by the time he's old enough to enlist," Ash countered. "And I think I need to thank you."

Anisimova frowned. "For what?"

"For this." She waved a hand to indicate the office and the talk. "The others have tried to talk to me about what happened, especially Mom. I know they understand. But they weren't there. More than that, they didn't know Loco like I did. But you did. You have been to battle with him. You know what sort of Marine he was because you helped make him who he was. But it goes beyond that. You were there when our friendship and professional relationship began and you've seen it grow over the years."

"Aw hell. Now you have me doing it." Anisimova reached up and swiped at her own tears. "We'll raise a glass to our friend this weekend. Now go home and spend some time with Jake. Most of all, quit beating yourself up over what happened. It wasn't your fault."

Ash stood and crossed to the door. Then she paused and straightened her shoulders. Anisimova was right. She needed to come to terms with what happened. It might take time to finally accept she wasn't responsible for what happened but it would come. She had to believe that. She'd never fully get over losing Talbot or Lucinda Ortega. But she would honor them. They were her friends, her family by choice. More importantly, they were Marines. It was time she remembered that.

Ooh-rah.

# 7

---

GOVERNMENT HOUSE
*Caspian Bay, Midlothian*

"QUIET!"

Jensen Vreman slammed his open palm down on the table, rattling glasses and startling those gathered. Almost as one, every head turned to him. Expressions ranged from surprised to angry, terrified to belligerent. Not that he cared. He had more important things to worry about than bruised egos. Their system faced the largest and most dangerous crisis of in memory. Worse, they were to blame. That left him to find a way to save not only their necks but his own.

Well, to be more accurate, Alexander Watchman was to blame for all the problems they now faced. But they allowed it to happen. Watchman went from useful tool to dangerous enemy a long time ago. Unfortunately, they didn't recognize the danger until it was too late. By then, he held the real power and used it to operate behind the scenes, manipulating politicians and businessmen however he wanted. When the Administrative Bureau realized the dangerous road he'd gone down with the Callusians, the noose had already tightened around their necks.

And no one did a damned thing.

Vreman knew the reasons. Some had been too scared of Watchman revealing what he knew about them, their families or their business dealings. Others approved of his actions and hoped to manipulate the Bureau into backing him against Fuercon and the others the system had supposedly been allied with. Instead of dealing with the threat Watchman presented to each of them, the men and women sitting around the table dealt with the situation by pointing fingers. While he understood—hell, he'd done his own share of finger-pointing—it solved nothing. Not in light of the latest revelations of the depravity of the Callusian war effort and not with Fuercon and her allies breathing down their necks, demanding satisfaction.

"This bickering accomplishes nothing." He made eye contact with each member of the council. Only a few held his gaze and he made note of those who looked away the quickest. Most were those he suspected of working with Watchman on his ill-advised scheme with the Callusians. One, however, surprised him by how quickly he looked away and Vreman made a mental note to look deeper into his relationship with the former Intelligence Czar. "The Fuerconese ambassador arrives in less than an hour. I have no doubt he brings with him a final demand from his government that we cooperate with the investigation into Watchman's activities or face the consequences. Are any of you willing to risk Harper and his allies declaring war on our system or, worse in many ways, pulling all military support from our sector? Do you want our people left helpless against the Callusians? Or are you going to do whatever it takes to save not only your own skins but our system?"

Silence filled the chamber. Vreman leaned back and waited. As he did, he made a mental bet with himself about who would speak first. One corner of his mouth twitched in an effort to smile when a small, painfully thin man midway down the table stood. He won the bet, if you could win when betting with yourself.

"You're making too much out of this, Vreman," Dominic Delespino said. "Fuercon will do nothing as long as we stand strong against their demands." Delespino glanced around the table and, seeing several heads nod in agreement, seemed to grow more confident. "Fuercon has no right to tell us how to run our government and it has no claim on any of our citizens. President Harper must not be allowed to dictate anything to us."

Vreman snorted in derision. As foolish as the argument was, the fact Delespino made it—and believed it—was even more so.

"They have every right to do just that, thanks to Watchman." Vreman activated the virtual keyboard in front of him and input a code. A moment later, the holo display above the table came to life. Every other person present gasped, a few even gagged, as images of what happened on Shennong appeared. "*This* gives them every right, at least in their minds, and this is why we can no longer refuse to discuss the situation with them."

"W-what do you mean?" Delespino paled and his hands shook before he shoved them into his pockets. He never had been a good card player and his nerves betrayed him yet again.

"We do what we were elected to do. We protect our system and our people. If that means working with the Fuerconese, we do so." Vreman leaned forward and steepled his hands in front of him. "Each of you know as well as I do that we need the Fuerconese and their allies to keep this system secure. Or would you rather we take our chances with the Callusians?"

Instead of answering, Delespino sat almost as quickly as the blood drained from his face. This time, Vreman made no attempt to hide his smile. Delespino had been a thorn in his side since joining the council. Perhaps his wife was right and it was time to clean house. Fuercon's demands certainly gave him the opportunity. It was risky, but if it prevented Fuercon from withdrawing its support—or worse—it was worth it.

At least he hoped so. Otherwise, he was about to make a very big, possibly fatal, mistake.

He entered another series of commands using the virtual keyboard. The holo display faded away. A moment later, the doors at the far end of the room opened and a dozen uniformed members of the capital guard entered. Hands on their sidearms, expressions grim, they took up positions around the room.

"What the hell is this?" Admiral Horace Boniface stood and looked defiantly around the room.

"This is called taking a proactive stance." Vreman nodded and the guards moved in. "Horace Boniface, Dominic Delespino, Charles Logaine and Sarah Lamar, you have been tied to the treasonous actions taken by Alexander Watchman. Investigators from the Intelligence Bureau discovered irrefutable evidence showing your complicity in his actions. Those actions, as well as your complicity, are in violation of the laws of our system. They also formed the basis of your conspiracy against our allies. Further, your actions gave aid to the enemy and cost untold lives. You will be held in custody until time to hand you over to Fuercon."

He stood, his expression cold. "Before that happens, you will be questioned by Major Rudolph. He will find out, one way or the other, if you know anything that will assist in locating Watchman."

Vreman smiled slightly as the four paled at Rudolph's name. Not that he blamed them. They knew the major's reputation. Before Watchman decided to cut his losses and flee the capital, Rudolph had been one of his closest associates. Watchman trained him and the younger man was as ruthless as the former Intelligence Czar. He was also loyal, to Vreman at least.

"You have as long as it takes to transport you to your cells to decide how you want this to play out. Know this, the rest of us will do whatever it takes to protect Midlothian, even if it means sacrificing the four of you. Watchman isn't here to save you. Cooperate or not, it's up to you."

He nodded and the guards quickly pulled those he indicated to their feet. They were roughly searched and then secured. Most stood silently, too stunned by the unexpected turn of events. Delespino, however, sputtered and struggled against the guard holding him. Vreman chuckled softly as the guard kicked him in the back of the knees and took him down.

"Hear me," Vreman said. "We played the odds by not taking Watchman in hand long ago. Each of us had our reasons, reasons we must now live with. That was our mistake. His was thinking he and his little cabal could operate behind our backs for their own benefit and against the system's best interests. Their actions turned our allies against us. We're lucky Fuercon and the others haven't already pulled their military presence from the system. Think about where we'd be if that were to happen.

"Worse, far worse, is that Watchman entered into an agreement with the Callusians to supply material and personnel, not to mention details about what Fuercon and the allies planned. If that isn't bad enough, they failed to live up to that agreement. Partly because the Fuerconese discovered the presence of certain of our naval officers onboard Callusian warships. Partly because the Callusian demands for more material couldn't be filled without raising our own suspicions.

"The result is that we are now squarely on the Callusians' radar. I shouldn't have to tell you how they feel about being betrayed. Nor should I have to tell you they will blame us, not Watchman, because we are in power now. All I know for sure is that they will want to make us, and the system, pay for Watchman's failure." He paused to give them time to digest what he said.

"Ask yourselves this: is it worth telling the Fuerconese ambassador we won't cooperate knowing what the Callusian bioweapon could do to any of our planets if it were used against us?"

Heads shook and voices murmured in the negative. That might change, but he already had a plan in place to deal with it if it did. If he was lucky, he'd have Watchman's head on a pike before that happened. That was probably the only thing that would mollify the Fuerconese short of handing the man over to them and that was something he didn't dare do. That bastard really did know where all the bodies were buried.

"Take them to Major Rudolph. Tell him he is to do whatever it takes to find out everything they know about Watchman." He waited as the guards led their prisoners out of the room. When the doors closed behind them, he turned his attention to the remaining members of the council. "Bethany, you are now our acting Secretary of State. When the Fuerconese ambassador arrives, inform him that we have taken a number of people into custody, including certain members of the government. Do not identify them. Tell the ambassador we will happily turn them over to him for transport to Fuercon after he presents the proper documentation and the Federal Court of Justice confirms everything is in order. That should buy Major Rudolph time to do what is necessary to get the information we need.

"Make no mistake, any of you. I will do whatever it takes to protect our system and its people. If that means cooperating with Fuercon and the others until this crisis is past, we will do so. There will be time later to make the appropriate response to any slight we suffer as a result." He sat once again and waited as the others did as well. "But for now, we must make sure we have allies who will stand to protect us against the Callusians. We use the time that buys us to build up our own navy into something more than the commercial enterprise it has become."

He paused and listened to the message coming in over his earbud.

"The ambassador will be here in approximately fifteen minutes. When you leave here, touch base with your contacts. Find Watchman for me. I don't give a fuck if he's alive or dead."

And he'd much prefer dead.

Vreman glanced around the table, wondering who would be the first to try to sell him out to the former intelligence czar. At least he felt confident Watchman was no longer in the system. Not that he didn't have his hooks into enough people locally he was still a danger. "Go." He waved for them to leave.

Hopefully, he'd bought himself and his home system time to play the odds without signing their death warrants.

---

*Fuerconese Embassy*
*Caspian Bay, Midlothian*

. . .

"WELL, that certainly wasn't what I expected."

Ambassador Morgan Izaguirre leaned back and crossed his legs. An hour and a half earlier, he'd been shown into the office of Midlothian's Secretary of State. Or, to be more accurate, the acting-Secretary of State. That had been the first of many surprises—for both of them. Fortunately for him and for Fuercon, he'd been a diplomat for more than ten years. Before that, he served in the Navy as an intelligence officer. That background helped keep his surprise at the sudden change in office holders from showing.

What he hadn't known, however, was what to expect from acting-Secretary Bethany Waas. When he first arrived, Izaguirre expected to be put off yet again, just as he had been every other time he met with his counterparts to discuss the situation concerning Watchman. He'd grown as tired as his government with the lip service Midlothian paid every time they promised their aid in finding Watchman. Lip service that had yet to turn into any action.

When Acting-Secretary Waas informed him members of the government, along with others, had been taken into custody, he had a more difficult time not letting his surprise show. Nor had he reacted when Waas assured him the prisoners would be transferred to his custody after all the legalities were met. Then it was his turn to reveal his own surprises and he once again said a quick prayer of thanks that Derek Harper was president and willing to do whatever was necessary to protect Fuercon and her allies.

"Which part?" Captain Reece Middleton leaned back and shook his head, his light blue eyes dancing with humor. "The part where you presented them with President Harper's ultimatum or the part where you had the paperwork ready the moment they asked for it? Or maybe it was the part where you said I had our ships in the system ready to move out and you'd already informed embassy personnel and their families to be ready to leave at a moment's notice?"

"Actually." Izaguirre all but rubbed his hands together gleefully. "It was all of that as well as when I named those of Watchman's co-

conspirators we'd already identified. I thought Waas was going to choke right there in front of me. I'm not sure what surprised her more: our knowing who the conspirators are or the fact she realized we have operatives—or they have traitors—placed high enough in the government to keep us informed about what's going on."

"True." Middleton lifted his mug in a toast. "I happened to like the part when you told her President Harper has authorized ships to translate here at their earliest convenience. You handled that bit masterfully. Waas couldn't take exception since you already informed her you had orders to withdraw all embassy staff and their dependents if the government continued to impede our investigation. Yet you could see her wondering if this was your way of giving a veiled threat that we were about to invade if they didn't start playing straight with us."

"Which is exactly what I wanted." The ambassador sipped his tea and then grinned. "I have to ask. Were you trying to make her piss her pants?"

Middleton chuckled. "I don't have any idea what you mean."

"Of course, you don't."

"Are you suggesting that my speculation that FleetCom might send Col. Shaw and the Devil Dogs with the ships was meant to be anything but what it was?"

Izaguirre shook his head and he looked at Middleton much as he would his own son when he'd done something unexpected and inspired, if not completely by the books. "She might not have pissed herself but she wanted to. I'll lay odds whoever was listening in on our conversation did as well."

"The government would do well to understand President Harper and FleetCom are done with their excuses and their betrayals. They either act like the allies they claimed to be or watch as we pull out and leave them to the tender mercies of the Callusians." Middleton's voice harshened and Izaguirre understood. They both had lost people they cared for since the renewal of hostilities.

"Reece, we will follow through. President Harper's made that perfectly clear. I suggest you put your ships on alert. I don't think the

Midlothians are foolish enough to try anything, especially now that they know we have reinforcements incoming. But then I never thought they would have been working with the Callusians." He waved the man's comment off. "I know the main government wasn't actively involved but only because they wanted plausible deniability. They let Watchman do what he wanted because it was easier than trying to take him down and risk their own secrets coming out."

"Agreed and consider it already done." The younger man checked his datapad before continuing. "Commander Khatri's last report confirms the increased alert status. She also reported that most of your peoples' dependents have been transported up."

"Good." The ambassador stood and moved to pour them each more coffee. "I hope the government here sees sense and turns Watchman's co-conspirators over to us. But the president is right. We have to be prepared for anything. Because of that, I'm going ahead and ordering all but essential personnel to evacuate to the ships until we know how this is going to play out. I'd appreciate it if you'd increase our Marine contingent at the embassy."

"Major Hoskins has his people ready. I'll give the order."

"Thank you." He returned to his seat behind his desk. "I'll have my report ready for President Harper within the hour."

"Then I'd best return to the ship to prepare my report for Fleet-Com. A courier ship is standing by to carry it home in case the transmission goes astray."

Izaguirre thanked him. The last dispatch from Fuercon included instructions to take every possible step to ensure messages between Midlothian and the home system did not go astray. Considering the fluidity of the situation and everything that could go wrong, Izaguirre didn't object. Hopefully, the precautions wouldn't be necessary.

"Hourly updates?" Middleton stood and straightened his uniform jacket.

"From each of us."

The captain nodded grimly. "I've ordered your shuttle to remain on standby, ready to cycle up its engines for immediate departure.

Your Marine escort knows to get you onboard at the first sign of trouble."

He didn't like it but Middleton was right. Which meant he had to make sure his wife was off-planet before anything happened.

If it happened.

# 8

---

"Mom, I don't want you to go."

Ash closed her eyes for a brief moment as she sought the right words to reassure him. In three days, she'd ship out. Despite all that needed to be done to prepare the regiment for the mission, she'd taken the morning off to be with her son. She needed the time as much as he did.

"I don't want to go."

It was the truth, at least partially. She didn't want to leave him. She understood his fear. She'd felt it every time one of her parents shipped out when she was growing up. That had been bad enough. She knew it was worse for Jake. Between her time at the penal colony as well as Lucinda's and Talbot's deaths, her son had lost a lot. What she couldn't explain was how she needed to do this to avenge their deaths and what had been done to her.

"Then don't." He and looked up at her, his expression serious.

Even though she preferred having this discussion at home, Ash knew it couldn't be put off. She glanced around, spotting a bench under a tree not far away. That would give them a little privacy from the rest of those enjoying the park that morning. At least she hoped so, just as she hoped she somehow managed to ease her son's concerns.

"Jake, you're old enough now to understand that sometimes we have to do things we don't want to do." When he nodded more than a little sullenly, she fought her smile. She'd said the same thing to him less than a week earlier when he wanted to skip school to go to work with her. He'd looked no happier then than he did now. "My job, just like Grandma's, is to help protect Fuercon. That means doing everything possible to keep everyone, and especially you and our family and friends, safe. If I stay here, I'm not doing everything I can."

"But you could get hurt."

Or worse.

She heard it even though he didn't say it.

"I could." She wouldn't lie to him. That was a lesson she'd learned from her parents. Each time one of them shipped out all those years ago, they promised they would do everything they could to come home to her and her siblings. Not once did they promise they would. When she asked about it once she was older, her father explained they didn't want her to remember the last thing they told her was a lie. It was a lesson she'd taken to heart. "And I have. But I promise to do everything I can not to get hurt."

"Why do you have to go?"

She slid an arm around his shoulders and drew him close. For a moment, she cradled him against her side. Then she bent her head and lightly brushed her lips against his hair. If she could promise him she'd always return, she would. But she couldn't. All she could do was try to reassure him and hope he understood—if not now, then later, when he was older.

"Jake, are you scared something's going to happen to me like it did to Aunt Lucinda and Uncle Kevin?"

He nodded his head against her side.

"Oh, baby." She wrapped her arms around him and pulled him onto her lap. The fact he didn't immediately squirm to get down told her how upset he was. "Can you look at me?"

He nodded again but it seemed to take forever for him to finally look up at her. Once he had, she lightly caressed his cheek with her left hand.

"Jake, I can't promise something won't happen to me or to your grandmother. We're Marines. More than that, we're Devil Dogs. That means we get sent where Fuercon needs us the most. But it also means we are the best at making sure we carry out our missions and come home safe. Unfortunately, sometimes bad things happen." She paused and considered just how much she should tell him. "But that doesn't mean we don't do everything we can to make sure we stay safe."

"But Aunt Lucinda and Uncle Kevin didn't come home." He sniffled once and ran a hand under his nose.

Ash gave him a quick hug and nodded. "Your Aunt Lucinda died trying to secure information that would save a lot of lives. Not only those under her command but many others. Your Uncle Kevin and the Marines with him died saving people too, me included. They died heroes. Just like you, I miss them a lot. But you know what?"

He shook his head.

"As long as we remember them and we tell others about them, they aren't completely gone. They live on in us." She reached up and fished the dog tags out from where they hung under her shirt. He watched as her fingers found Lucinda's tag by touch, separating it from the others on the chain around her neck. "I wear Aunt Lucinda's dog tag, just like you wear Uncle Kevin's, to honor them and their sacrifice. But I want you to remember something."

Several somethings, actually.

"What?"

"They both loved you. I know they were here for you as much as they could be while I was on Tarsus." She fought to keep the anger from her voice as she remembered the two years spent at the penal colony. She'd missed so much of her son's early years as a result. "I know they would give anything to be with you now. But they would tell you exactly what I am. They'd tell you they did their duty as Marines and would do it again, even knowing what would happen."

For a long time, they sat in silence. When Jake finally wiggled off her lap and onto the bench at her side, she waited. She wanted to reassure him some more but she knew the next move had to be his. All she hoped was she was ready for it, whatever it might be.

"Promise to be careful?" He looked up at her and she fought the urge to laugh. He wore the same expression her mother did when asking her the same thing.

"I promise." Inspiration hit and she reached under her shirt for the dog tags hanging on the chain around her neck. Jake watched as she carefully removed two of the tags. "Jake, I'm making you a promise right now that I will do everything I can to return home safely from this mission. To prove it, I want you to hold onto these for me. This one." She held up the newer of the two dog tags. "This was your Aunt Lucinda's dog tag. Her parents asked me to wear it after she died. It is one way I honor her."

She closed his hand over the tag, waiting until he nodded.

"This dog tag." She held up the second one. "This one belonged to your great-grandfather. Grandma's father. He died not too long before you were born. I want you to hold onto both of these, wear them with Uncle Kevin's dog tag, until I get home. Can you do that for me?"

He slid off the bench and stood before her. One corner of her mouth twitched as he did a credible imitation of bracing to attention. Then he pulled the chain with Talbot's dog tag out from under his shirt. With Ashlyn's help, he secured the two tags on it before closing his hand around the three tags.

"I will." He stood there, his small hand wrapped around the dog tags. Then he looked at her and grinned. "This means you have to come home."

She smiled and nodded, praying this wasn't the mission to break his trust in her and in the Corps.

"Can I go to your ship with you tomorrow?"

Ash laughed and reached out to ruffle his hair. Then she glanced at her watch and stood. Like it or not, it was time to get him home and for her to get back to work.

"Maybe not tomorrow, but you can come visit me there before I ship out." She'd make the time, somehow. The taskforce was shipping out in three days. Her orders were for her to transition onboard the next morning. Until they shipped out, she knew there wouldn't be enough hours in the day to get everything done. But she wouldn't disappoint her son. Not if she could help it.

"Promise?"

"I promise." That was one promise she would keep, no matter what. "I'll ask Grandma or Grandpa to bring you, son. We'll also talk every day until I leave."

"Good." He gave a decisive nod.

"Now, before I report back to duty, how about stopping at Noomi's for a treat?"

He grinned and threw his arms around her waist. Then he raced forward, dragging her behind him. Laughing, Ash quickened her pace to keep up. Not that she blamed him. Noomi's had the best pastries around.

---

Colonel Rico Santiago closed his eyes and inhaled deeply. He'd not been surprised to learn Ashlyn Shaw wanted to see him. Not only had they worked together closely since she returned from her last mission, going over the data recovered and discussing its possible ramification but there were still questions surrounding why she and those under her command had been set up on the Arcterus mission. The problem was the latter investigation continued to go slowly, much too slowly for either of them. Unfortunately, those involved who had already been arrested weren't talking and the one person who might hold all the answers couldn't.

And he knew that was the person Shaw wanted to talk to him about.

A knock sounded and his office door slid open. By the time he stood and moved around his desk, Ashlyn Shaw entered. As the door slid shut behind her, Santiago grinned and extended his hand. She took it and motioned to the chairs in front of his desk, one brow arched in question. He gave a nod and then shook his head when she continued to stand.

"Knock it off, Ash. Sit." He had time in grade over her, as she'd reminded him. But they were friends and, behind closed doors, didn't need to fall back on formality. At least he hoped not. "What can I do for you?"

"You know I'm shipping out in a couple of days."

It wasn't really a question, but he nodded any way. "I do."

"Two things, then. First, tell me about the Intel staff you've assigned to the mission."

One brow arched in surprise. He had expected another question from her. Not that it wouldn't come. It reassured him, however, that she put the mission first. Of course, she always did. But he was one of the few who knew how hard that had been at times for her after what happened on Arterus and afterwards.

"It's a good team." One of his best, actually. If the taskforce was going anywhere except Midlothian, he wouldn't be sending them. But if things went the way he expected, he wanted them handing not only any prisoners but any data secured during the course of the mission. "Major Khan is a skilled interrogator but even more skilled at ferreting out data that has been hidden. Lt. Okumura follows the proverbial dots like a hunting hound. Cpl. Zimm is the muscle. He doesn't say much and is intimidating as hell. But his strength is in spotting inconsistencies before the quarry can figure out how to cover them up."

"Good." She gave a decisive nod. "How are they in battle situations?"

He understood why she asked. Khan and Zimm were Marines. That put them technically under her command should the proverbial shit hit the fan. She needed to know if she could rely on them or if she needed to relegate them to Damage Control should the mission go south.

"Khan and Zimm came up through the ranks, Ash. They know how to handle themselves. As for Okumura, if things go bad, she can back up helm or weaponry."

"Good." Another nod. "Now, anything about the mission you can tell me that wasn't in the briefing pack?" She angled in her chair so she could look at him. Then she stretched out her long legs and crossed them at the ankles.

"You'll have an updated packet waiting for you by morning." He lifted a hand to stop her from interrupting. "The gist of it is that Harper's latest message seems to have put the fear of God into the members of the Administrative Bureau. We aren't supposed to know this yet, but Vreman took steps less than a week ago in an attempt to place them in a better position by the time the taskforce—they aren't to be told it is more than that—arrives. Our sources tell us several members of the Bureau were taken into custody and Vreman made it clear he will use whatever means necessary to locate Watchman. The goal now is to find the bastard before he does. None of my people doubt Watchman will be dead if Vreman finds him before we do. The Bureau, and all too many others, can't afford for the man to fall into our hands."

"Are we going to be walking into a repeat of the Savitar VI debacle?"

He shook his head. "I don't think so." At least he hoped not. "Everything we're seeing from Midlothian right now is that they are doing their best to not only cover their respective asses but make sure we don't pull our military support from the system. The government there knows what will happen if we do. It wouldn't take long for the Callusians to roll through and none of them want that to happen."

"Then they should have kept Watchman and his cronies in hand." She all but ground it out, not that he blamed her. They might never know how many died as a result of that betrayal. "Are there special instructions about what your people aren't to do while in-system?"

He chuckled softly. She really did know him too well. "They aren't to get caught as they try to hack the intelligence files and anything else they track down that's related to Watchman and what's been going on there where the Callusians are concerned."

"I'm sure we can arrange something to keep the Midlothians

distracted while they do their work." Ashlyn's smile was all predatory hunter, not that he blamed her.

"I do believe Harper and Nelms have that well in hand." His smile matched hers and she chuckled softly.

"And Moreau?"

He didn't answer immediately. Even though he'd expected the question, he still hadn't decided on an answer. Part of him wanted to reassure her they were making progress where the would-be assassin was concerned. The last thing he wanted was for her to be distracted during her mission. But he also knew better than to lie to her and telling her they were making progress would be doing just that. The woman lying in a secure cell turned into a hospital room several floors beneath his office might have called herself Evan Moreau the last few years, but they had no clue who she'd been before then. Nor did they know why she tried to kill President Harper. His gut told him it was all tied to the war and the trouble with the Midlothians, but he didn't know for sure.

"Medically, there has been little to no change." That was the easy part. Besides, he knew Ash tied into the video feed from the woman's cell at least once a day. Not that he blamed her. Ash had taken the shot meant for Harper. That gave her a very personal reason to want to know all there was about Moreau. "After the change in her condition was noted, the CMO reviewed the records of everyone working her case. Let's just say he wasn't happy with what he found. There is a new team monitoring her now and the CMO has taken a personal hand in her treatment."

Ash nodded and he relaxed a little. She already knew that much and she seemed to approve of the steps taken.

"There has been an increase in brain activity. From what the doctors are saying, they agree with your observations before you left on that last mission. Moreau is aware of what is going on around her. As a result, the treatment team is under orders to discuss nothing but her condition and what steps they are taking whenever they are in the room with her."

"That has to be frustrating the hell out of her."

Ashlyn's smile sent a chill down his spine.

"Let's hope so." His smile matched hers. "She is being monitored around the clock, as you know." He waited until she nodded once. "And there has been signs of her regaining at least minimal movement in one hand. She's shown involuntary responses to stimuli on one foot. But nothing else. At least not so far and the medical team doesn't believe she can be faking it. As the CMO said, no one is that good of an actress. But they are keeping a very close eye on her."

"Guards?"

"One is stationed outside the cell. A second guard is present whenever anyone from the member of the medical team is in with her. There are no other prisoners in the section with her and the section is on full lockdown. Other precautions, some we haven't informed the medicals of, have been put in place as well."

He didn't explain and she didn't ask. He appreciated that. Not only did it give her plausible deniability if anyone should ask, but she probably had a good idea what he meant. She served with him early in her career. That meant she had a good idea how his mind worked.

"Any progress on tracking down who she really is?"

He shook his head, his expression grim.

"No, but we are still digging through everything we can find on her. I've never found an alias as well put together as hers. Someone had not only the money but the talent to erase her from the DNA files, scrub her identity and make sure there is nothing we can tag, at least not easily, to find out who she is. The medicals are working with us to isolate anything in her genetic makeup that might help us. But we will find something. No alias is perfect and that includes hers." He leaned over and rested a hand on her arm, waiting until she blew out a breath.

"Ash, she isn't going to get away with what she did. I promise." He didn't care what it took. He would find out who Moreau was and why she targeted Harper and, unless he was very wrong, Ashlyn herself. "And I will let you know the moment we have anything concrete. You have my word."

"I know, Rico." She gave a slight smile. "I can't believe she just happened to choose the Midlothian Embassy as her perch when she tried to kill Harper because of its location. There were other buildings in the area, ones with easier means of entry, than the embassy. The fact she managed to get inside the grounds, and with a weapon, convinces me she'd been there before. I can't help thinking someone inside was helping her. If that's the case, we need to know who before something else happens."

"Agreed." He stood and moved around his desk. He opened the lap drawer and pulled out a file, one normally kept under lock and key. Even though he didn't offer it to Ash, he used it to make his next point. "These are my orders from President Harper. He's made it very clear he wants to know what happened and why. The members of your regiment and Capital Security are the visible presence he wanted to let the Midlothians know we are keeping them under watch. My people are doing everything we can to covertly keep an eye on them. It is amazing what folks say when they think no one is listening."

"All right." She checked her wrist unit and stood. "I need to run. I've got a briefing with my regimental commanders and their XOs. I appreciate the time, Rico."

"Any time, Ash." He walked with her to the door. "I will find the answers to your questions."

"I know." She gave him a smile. "Let's hope your people on the mission are as good as you said. I have a feeling we're going to need them before it's all over."

"They are. Bring them, and yourself, home safe."

He watched as she left his office. Then he turned back to his desk. There was a great deal to do and not enough hours in the day to do it. Time was running short and he prayed they found the answers necessary to not only get to the bottom of the Midlothian conspiracy but to end the war with the Callusians once and for all.

---

"ARE YOU ALL RIGHT?"

Ashlyn straightened and smiled at her mother. Elizabeth stood in the doorway to the bedroom. Dressed in loose lounging pants and a soft knit tunic, the woman bore little resemblance to the capable Marine Ash knew her to be. Instead, she was the worried mother and grandmother. Not that Ash blamed her. They both knew how many ways this mission could go sideways without warning.

"I'm fine." She gave a slight shrug. "Jake's having a hard time about my leaving."

"And that makes it even harder for you."

Ash nodded.

Elizabeth crossed the room. As she sat on the edge of the bed, she patted the mattress and waited until Ash joined her. Then she reached for Ashlyn's hand. For a while, they sat in silence, two mothers worried about their children even if for different reasons.

"You were about the same age when you asked me not to go on a mission. I don't know if you remember." Elizabeth spoke softly, her gaze on their joined hands.

"I don't remember," Ash admitted.

"Your father was off-planet at the time. FleetCom moved up the departure date for the Devil Dogs. You and your brother were going to be left here, with Marie, until Abe returned home. It was the first time we'd both been gone at the same time. It wouldn't be the last, but it was the hardest on you, especially since I'd only been home a few weeks."

"I think I remember." Her brow knitted. "There was something else about that time. Something beyond you shipping out early."

Elizabeth nodded, her expression grim. "We didn't tell you what happened on that last mission. But you knew something bad had happened. You never asked what. Maybe you knew we wouldn't tell you. Not that it stopped you from keeping an eagle eye on me."

The pieces slowly fell into place. Ash remembered how, not long after her return from the penal colony, Elizabeth told her she understood at least some of how she felt. Without going into detail, she explained she'd been captured on a mission. While it wasn't the same as being betrayed by those she trusted or spending two years in a penal colony, she knew what it was to be a prisoner, abused by her captors. Had that been what Ash sensed so long ago?

"Mama." Emotion roughened her voice.

Elizabeth smiled sadly and slid an arm around her shoulders, holding her close. "It was the hardest thing I'd ever done to leave you that next mission. But I knew if I didn't, I'd never be effective as a Marine again. I owed it to the Marines I served with, and to those who died on the previous mission, to obey orders. I owed it to myself —and to you and the rest of the family—to as well. It was the only way I knew to return to myself."

"I wouldn't have understood then. I do know." And she hoped the day came when Jake would as well.

"And Jake will as well." Elizabeth paused and Ash knew she was considering her next words. "He's worried about you and he's scared you might not come home. That's natural, especially after everything you've been through the last few years. But he knows you have to go and, judging from the way he was hanging onto the new dog tags, he's going to hold you to your promise." Now she grinned. "I left you one of my dog tags that mission."

"I remember. I also remember wearing it every day until you returned home and I could give it back to you."

"You and are two of a kind, child. You need to trust your father and sister to take good care of Jake while you're gone."

"I do. Just as I trust you to." Hopefully, she'd be back home before Elizabeth shipped out. She didn't like having the division, much less the regiment, split among different sectors. Not when she knew the final push to end the war was coming.

"Is there anything I can do to help you pack?"

"No. I'm about done." She looked around her room and her eyes fell on a small package resting on the bedside table. She stood and moved to it. "I told Jake we'd talk every day before we ship out. Will you make sure he gets this the next day?" She handed the package to her mother.

Elizabeth weighed the box in her hands. Then she nodded. "Of course."

"Then there is just one more thing. He wants to come to the ship. Can you or Dad bring him day after tomorrow? I'll let you know when is best."

"We can." In the distance, one of the antique clocks struck eleven. "You need to get some rest."

"Yeah." She glanced around the room, taking stock. "I think I've done all I can tonight and bed sounds good."

Elizabeth gave her a quick hug and then stepped back, looking her square in the eye. "Jake's going to be fine, Ash. Don't worry about him."

"I'll always worry about him, just like you and Dad worry about me and the sibs."

Her mother chuckled and nodded. "Get some rest. I'll see you at breakfast."

Ash watched as her mother left the room, closing the door behind her. Then she turned her attention back to her duffle. She'd finish packing and turn in for the night. Morning and the realities of duty would come all too soon.

## 9

---

*Government Center*
*Caspian Bay, Midlothian*

Jensen Vreman fought the urge to curse long and hard. In all his years as a member of the Administrative Bureau, he'd never felt so helpless. No, that wasn't right. He'd never felt the noose tightening so inexorably around his neck. It might still be only figuratively, but it was only a matter of time before it became reality. He knew it. Unfortunately, he wasn't sure what he could do about it.

Damn Alexander Watchman! This was all his fault. If they were in a room together, Vreman would kill him. There'd be no mercy. There couldn't be. Watchman was why they found themselves in their current unenviable position. If only they knew where he was. Unfortunately, Watchman was living up to his reputation of being the best intelligence officer Midlothian had ever had. He used that knowledge to disappear and the Bureau didn't know if he was still in the system.

"You're sure?" Zander Felchin asked.

Vreman looked at one of the Bureau's newest members. Felchin and three others had been appointed less than a fortnight ago to replace the four he'd ordered arrested for conspiring with Watchman. Of the four, Felchin seemed the least able to accept the difficult position Midlothian found itself in. Not that Vreman blamed him. In the younger man's shoes, he'd probably feel the same way. Unfortunately, that attitude did little to help just then.

"We are," Bethany Waas, the newly confirmed Secretary of State, said. She glanced at her notes. When she looked up, Vreman nodded for her to continue. "We knew Fuercon and the other members of the alliance wouldn't waste much time in sending ships here. The ambassador made it clear he was under orders to either secure our cooperation in the hunt for Watchman and all those who worked with him or the allies were pulling their support. The Chairman warned us not to take the threat too lightly. Unfortunately, we didn't expect them to act quite so quickly."

"Nor did we expect the message to be quite so clear." Vreman activated the holo display over the conference table. A moment later, someone down the table gasped in surprise. Not that he blamed them. He'd done much the same thing as he watched a replay of the images of the Fuerconese ships entering the system. His insides had turned to water until he remembered they were still, at least technically, allies. "As you can see, Fuercon is making their message clear by sending more than enough ships to remove every one of their citizens, not to mention other allied personnel and dependents. Now think about this, there is enough firepower in-system to take over without any trouble. Our desire to focus on commerce rather than military strength has left us at an extreme disadvantage."

And that was putting it mildly.

"What do they want?" Santos Reyes asked from the opposite end of the table.

Vreman studied the Labor Secretary for a moment. Reyes looked like someone's jolly and harmless grandfather. The truth was far from that.

"We will find out soon enough. Secretary of State Marc Nelms is onboard the flagship and will be transporting planetside within the hour. Ambassador Izaguirre sent word shortly before I called this briefing that a formal audience with Bethany was being requested. I think it fair to say our time has run out."

"Do you really believe they will try to force the issue?" Hollis Browning asked from her place two seats to Vreman's left.

He looked at the woman and for not the first time wondered what plane of existence she occupied. It certainly wasn't the reality of their current situation. She seemed either unable or incapable of believing the Fuerconese and their allies would take exception to what Watchman and others had planned with the Callusians. After all, to Browning's way of thinking, it had been a purely business matter and had nothing to do with the treaties Midlothian had signed with Fuercon and the allied systems.

And that was exactly the sort of thinking that led them to their current situation. For far too long, the leadership had refused to see there was more to be considered than the bottom line. Controlling commerce in this part of the galaxy was all well and good but it wouldn't save them from the Callusians, especially not with their new weapon, or from Fuercon's fury.

"Bethany?"

She nodded once to Vreman. Then she pushed back her chair and stood. As she did, the Chairman smiled slightly. This was a different woman than the one most of those on the Bureau knew. Until he'd named her as Acting-Secretary of State, she seemed content to stay in the background, rarely offering any opinion unless asked. Vreman knew it was a mask, once she carefully crafted to keep her fellow members of the Bureau from looking too closely. If the Chairman could point to any one failure by Watchman, Vreman would point to the woman. As Watchman worked to manipulate the Bureau into doing what he wanted, she'd worked behind the scenes to assist Vreman and others to safeguard not only the Bureau but the system as well.

"They don't have to force the issue, Ms. Browning. Thanks to our media, it won't be long before everyone in the system realizes not only that Fuercon and her allies have sent a delegation here but they did so with a force large enough to be termed a taskforce. That alone is proof they will do whatever they feel necessary to protect their interests. Are you willing to risk not complying with what they want?"

"Are we willing to give in and let them dictate how we govern our system?" Browning countered.

Vreman stopped Waal before she could respond. "What do you think will happen if we refuse to cooperate with them, Hollis?" He spoke softly, almost as if he might be discussing the weather. Little did Browning realize he was anything but relaxed.

"Nothing. This is all a show. They wouldn't dare try to force us to act. The rest of the allies wouldn't stand for it."

He found it hard to believe the woman could be that foolish. "This isn't the former administration we're dealing with, Hollis." He held the woman's gaze for a moment before glancing around the table. "Derek Harper is a man of action. He's proven that time and again since taking office. He has also put people in positions of power who believe the way he does. So, to answer your question, I have no doubt Ambassador Izaguirre is here to deliver an ultimatum. We either turn over everyone and everything we have that is connected with Watchman and his machination with the Callusians or we will very shortly find ourselves without any allied protection. I don't know about you, but I do not want to leave our system open to attack from the Callusians."

"And do not discount the potential for the Callusians to turn their attention to our system," Wass said as she moved to the Chairman's side. "I have received word from operatives loyal to the Chairman that they are not pleased with the way Watchman has dropped out of sight or with the fact we are not continuing to live up to his bargain with them. I have no doubt the only reason they haven't already sent a strikeforce against us is because Fuercon and the other systems have been protecting us. Remove that protection and we not only become the proverbial sitting duck but there is little we can do about it."

"But they can't afford a multi-front war." Reyes spoke with such confidence Vreman wondered if he actually bought into Browning's alternate reality.

"What multi-front war?" he snapped. "If we can't protect our home system, how in the hell are we going to go to war with anyone?" Disgust filled him. It was no wonder they were in the trouble they were. Too many of the Bureau lived in worlds of their own making, worlds that had little to do with reality. "Do you honestly believe we could repel the ships currently in our system with our merchant navy? Even if we could, do you think they would then be able to stand against the Callusians? If you do, I suggest you find your nearest mental health professional and check yourselves in for long term treatment."

Was this why Watchman worked behind the scenes for his own agenda. Had the Bureau been so ineffectual, the Intelligence Czar saw his actions as the only way to save the system? While he could see it, he couldn't condone it. Not after seeing what the Callusians had done on Shennong. He didn't care what it took or how many political asses he had to kiss, he wouldn't let that happen to Midlothian or any of her holdings.

"How dare you!" Reyes started to rise only to drop back onto his chair when Vreman glared at him.

"I dare because I will not sacrifice our homeworld just to save that bastard Watchman!" His nostrils flared as he drew in a deep, cleansing breath. He held it for a moment before exhaling. "Bethany and I will be on hand to greet Secretary of State Nelms when he arrives at the spaceport. When we formally meet, I will agree to handing over the prisoners we already have in custody." He lifted a hand to hold off any protests. "However, they will have to prove their right to take those prisoners in our courts. That should buy us some time. I suggest we make good use of it and find that bastard Watchman."

With that, he turned and left the conference room, Waas on his heels. As the doors shut behind them, he prayed Major Rudolph managed to learn something from the prisoners and soon. Time was running out.

Damn Watchman and those fools who still protected him!

HE CHECKED the door and activated the security screen. As he did, he fought the urge to beat his head against the wall. While he understood Vreman's worry, he knew it was misplaced. Harper and the rest of the Fuerconese might bluster and threaten, but they would never follow through. It just wasn't in them. The real danger was in giving in to them and siding against the Callusians.

It was now a matter of doing whatever it took to save his own skin. Only then could he do anything to help his homeworld. And if that meant working with the Devil, he'd do so. Besides, the Devil knew all his secrets and had already shown he had no qualms using them against him.

"It's me," he said over a secured link a few minutes later. "There's been a development we didn't anticipate."

"Tell me."

He frowned, wondering for not the first time if he was doing the right thing. The blank screen might hide the appearance of the person on the other end of the call, but he knew that voice all too well. It was a voice that sent chills down the spines of men much braver than he.

"A Fuerconese taskforce is in-system as we speak. Secretary of State Nelms is onboard one of the ships. Vreman and Waas are sure he is here to give Harper's final demands concerning any alliances with or support given to the Callusians. The best case scenario is that he can stall them for a while. Worst case is that they pull all personnel and dependents out of the system, taking with them all military support as well."

"I see." Silence followed and he waited, wondering if the call had been ended. "Don't panic and don't give Vreman or the others reason to suspect you. I'll be in touch."

This time there was no doubt he ended the call. Reyes leaned forward and slowly pounded his head against the wall. He was caught between the proverbial rock and the hard place and saw no way out. Not unless he managed to locate Watchman. But did he dare risk turning the former spy chief in?

Damn it, there were too many players in this game and little chance of winning.

# LINE IN THE SAND

# 10

*ATLANTIS RISING, FLAGSHIP*
*First Fleet, Fuerconese Navy*
*Midlothian space*

ADMIRAL MIRANDA TREMAYNE stood in the middle of the flag bridge
and allowed a small smile to lift the corners of her mouth. She'd
commanded her fair share of state-of-the-art battle cruisers over the
course of her career. They all paled in comparison with the *Atlantis
Rising*. The ship was fresh off her shakedown cruise and it was all
hers. Well, hers and her flag captain and it made a very clear statement to anyone standing in her way.

Or it should if they had an ounce of common sense in them.

"They're ready for you, Admiral."

She turned and nodded to Lt. Stahl in appreciation. "Ask the Mess
to send up coffee and tea for everyone. We may be a while."

"Aye, Admiral."

Tremayne drew a bracing breath and crossed to her ready room.
As she did, she prepared herself. Waiting for her were her senior officers as well as Secretary of State Marc Nelms. Since leaving Fuercon,

they met twice a day to discuss how best to deal with the Midlothian government. President Harper and FleetCom's orders were clear. But it was up to them to find a resolution to the situation that wouldn't lead to leaving the system open to Callusian attack.

"Atten-shun!"

Ashlyn Shaw hadn't finished the order before those gathered around the table pushed back and stood. As they braced to attention, the colonel stepped to the head of the table. Then she, too, snapped to attention. As she did, Secretary of State Nelms stood, waiting respectfully for Tremayne to join them.

"Be seated," the admiral said as she took her seat. "Let me begin by confirming what some of you already know. As of 1400 hours, we split the fleet into two parts. Captain Earhardt commands the reserve force. He will hold it outside of the system, beyond detection range and in stealth until such time as it is needed—if it is needed. No mention of the reserve force is to be made over any open comm or in public until further notice. Is that understood?"

She waited until each person present indicated they not only understood but would follow the order.

"While this is supposed to be a diplomatic mission, we are not going to drop our guard. Members of the Midlothian government have already shown they are willing to betray not only Fuercon's best interests but the best interests of our allies as well. It is up to them to prove they can be trusted. We will not risk being betrayed again." She glanced to her right. "Colonel Shaw."

Ashlyn stood. As she did, the holo display at the far end of the room came to life. One half showed the fleet's current position in relation to the capital planet. Also highlighted were system defense, sensor and comms platforms. The other half of the display showed similar information from the Savitar VI System upon the arrival of Taskforce Liberator after the attack on Shennong.

"Thank you, Admiral." She sipped from her coffee mug before continuing. "I won't insult any of us by saying the situation we face right now is the same as what we faced when the taskforce arrived in the Savitar VI System. I hope none of you ever have to face what we did on that mission. The biotoxin used by the Callusians decimated the planet. It will be months, perhaps years or even decades before the planet can be settled again. When I say we were lucky the enemy failed to successfully use the biotoxin against any of our ships, I'm putting it mildly." She entered a command and the second half of the display changed to show a list of Midlothians FleetIntel confirmed to be working against Fuercon's best interest.

"We must not forget that members of the Midlothian government not only aided and abetted the enemy but that they actively plotted against Fuercon and our true allies. They have provided the enemy with technology, finances and 'advisors', all with the ultimate goal of defeating the alliance we've built against the Callusians. While it's true the Administrative Bureau did not know exactly when we would arrive—or what in what numbers—it knows we're coming. That means we must be on the lookout for the potential for betrayal.

"I briefed Admiral Tremayne and Secretary Nelms earlier concerning my recommendations as Marine CO. Those recommendations begin with immediately instituting the new protocols adopted by FleetCom to combat the spread of the biotoxin. That means keeping each compartment secured and increased environmental monitoring. That will help slow the spread of the biotoxin should it somehow be introduced onto any of our ships. My other recommendations include limiting who is allowed to go dirtside, sending full Marine guard details with those who do and all Marine details being in full battle rattle when off-ship. It might seem like overkill, but I assure you it is necessary. We are at war and Midlothians has thrown support to our enemy. It is time to show them we will no longer sit by and allow them to play both ends against the middle."

She input another command and the holo screen changed to display images from Shennong. Gasps and curses greeted the change and she gave them a chance to die down before continuing.

"Ladies and gentlemen, this is what the enemy can and will do. There is no doubt they will use the biotoxin against us given the chance We must be prepared for that possibility.

"But there is another possibility we must also be prepared for. We know Alexander Watchman and others in the government entered into an agreement with the enemy to offer them support against Fuercon and her allies. That agreement has been put in danger by its discovery. Our sources tell us the government has not sent any further assistance or aid to the Callusians since President Harper put it on notice that we will not turn a blind eye to what they were doing. That presents the very real possibility that the Callusians will decide to make an example of this system. By forcing Midlothian's hand with regard to Alexander Watchman and those helping him, we have put the Callusian gunsights directly on Midlothian and President Harper does not want the innocents here to pay the price."

"Colonel Shaw is correct." Secretary of State Marc Nelms stood and studied the images from Shennong for a moment before continuing. "But make no mistake. If the government here refuses to cooperate or if Admiral Tremayne and I feel they are actively working to impede our attempts to locate Watchman and those who assisted him, we will not only remove allied citizens from the system but we will withdraw all allied military support. None of us want to leave the system open to attack but we will not risk our own systems to protect them while their government actively works against us.

"That is the message I will deliver to the Administrative Bureau later today. President Harper set a deadline for their cooperation at three planetary days. If they do not turn over all they know about Watchman's association with the Callusians, not to mention any prisoners they have and all data they have collected regarding the investigation, in that time, we will proceed with our withdrawal."

"Begging your pardon, Mr. Secretary," Captain Raoul Kohler said from his place further down the table. "You didn't mention turning Watchman over."

Nelms inclined his head, his expression serious. "I did not because our intel from the planet is to the effect that they don't know where he is. Most of the Administrative Bureau appears to be operating under the belief he fled the system before we demanded his arrest. However, we have solid intelligence that not only is Watchman still in the system but that he is still on the capital planet. That is where

Major Khan and his people come into play. They will be working their magic to locate Watchman while Ambassador Izaguirre and I meet with the government."

"And that is where we come in," Tremayne said. "While the negotiations are taking place, shuttles will be running between the capital planet and our ships. The sole purpose for that, at least as far as the Midlothians are concerned, is to bring our people onboard in preparation for a withdrawal. While that is true, up to a point, these shuttles are actually a diversion. We want the Midlothians focused on them while our LACS are busy doing something we aren't going to announce. We are taking a page from Admiral Collins' playbook in the Savitar VI System. We'll be launching our own defense platforms and passive scanner arrays in-system to alert us to any potential enemy approach. We will not be caught unprepared.

"From this point forward and until we leave the system, we are on alert. All essential operations will be covered not only by duty staff but by their back-ups. We are now on compartmental discipline. If I hear of one slip up, there will be hell to pay. I'm not losing anyone, much less a ship, to this biotoxin. Am I clear?"

"Yes, ma'am!"

"Going forward, we will meet three times a day. If everything goes as planned, we will be in and out of the system in less than a week. No matter what the government's decision, our next stop will be our home system where we will either leave our citizens currently located here or we will leave our prisoners before joining the push to finally take the war directly to the enemy."

"Ooh-rah," Ash said softly and Tremayne smiled.

"Ooh-rah indeed, Colonel." She glanced around the table, letting her gaze rest on each person present. "In all likelihood, this will be an easy mission and nothing will go wrong. However, let's not let ourselves be lulled into a false sense of security. If something looks or feels wrong, don't ignore it. Let's not take any unnecessary risks."

An hour later, she dismissed those gathered. When she looked up from her notes a few moments later, it didn't surprise her to find Nelms still at his place at the table. Then she saw the other two who remained and shook her head, a rueful smile tugging at the corners of her mouth. She should have expected Ashlyn to remain, but she was still having a hard time accepting the fact Sergeant Major Anisimova was present as well. The Corps' senior non-commissioned officer had reported to the flagship shortly before they left the system. Her orders were clear and came directly from General Okafor. She was Ashlyn's acting senior non-com until they returned to Fuercon. That was all the time the colonel had to decide who would replace Talbot.

"Mr. Nelms, your shuttle will be ready to depart in half an hour," Tremayne said as she set her datapad to one side.

"Excellent. Thank you. I can't help feeling the sooner we deal with this situation, the better."

"Colonel, what about his escort?"

"The good sergeant major has hand-picked his escort, ma'am." Ash grinned at Anisimova and Tremayne narrowed her eyes suspiciously. "I added my own twist to it."

The look Anisimova gave Ash had Tremayne biting her lip to keep from laughing. Whatever Ash had done, the sergeant major didn't appreciate it.

"Really now?" Tremayne arched one red brow in question.

"Ambassador, Sgt. Major Anisimova will be leading your escort. It will consist of half a dozen Marines from the Devil Dogs and Warlords. All will be in battle armor and two will be in heavy armor. My orders from both General Okafor and President Harper are clear. Your escort is to be armed and armored at all times, no matter what the Midlothians say. They are tasked first with keeping you safe. After that, their priorities are to get the ambassador to safety. That means, sir, if the sergeant major tells you to do something, you will do so. Otherwise, I assure you she will take whatever steps she feels necessary to make sure she carries out our orders."

"What Colonel Shaw means is I will have one of the heavies throw you over his shoulder and carry you out of danger if necessary, sir," Anisimova said.

"Heard and understood." He grinned at them both before turning serious. "You forget I spent almost twenty years in the Navy before I was beached due to injury. My respect for Marines in general and your regiment in particular, Colonel, means I will do as you say."

"Thank you, sir." She turned her attention to Tremayne. "With your permission then, ma'am, the sergeant major and I have some matters to deal with before the Secretary and his escort leave the ship."

"Of course." She stood and returned their salutes. "Colonel, join me for dinner tonight."

"Yes, ma'am. Have your aide comm me with the details."

"I'm not sure which of them scares me more, Miranda," Nelms said with a light laugh as the hatch slid shut behind them.

"I know what you mean. Anisimova was senior non-com on the colonel's first mission out of the Academy. She took Ashlyn under her wing and they've been close ever since then. To say they are made from the same mold is understating the case." She returned to her seat. "Now, Marc, let's see if we can anticipate what Vreman and his people are going to say when you meet with them later today."

---

"ANY QUESTIONS?" Ashlyn leaned back and stretched her arms high over her head, stretching.

Edita Anisimova shook her head, her expression thoughtful. "A suggestion is all."

Ash didn't shake her head even though she wanted to. She had no doubt the sergeant major had more than one "suggestion". The blonde had not been pleased to learn she would be leading the ambassador's security team. The only thing that had mollified her was learning Ash would remain onboard the *Atlantis Rising*. Even that, however, hadn't stopped her from telling the colonel she knew exactly what Ash was doing and she didn't like it one bit.

"Go ahead."

As she waited, Ash admitted to herself it was strange to have their roles reversed. When they first served together, Ash was fresh out of the Academy. Like so many newly minted officers, she'd felt invincible. At least she knew enough to listen to her gunnery sergeant. Because of that, she'd learned a great deal from Anisimova that first tour. The blonde helped shape her into the officer she was today. But now it was her command and even though Anisimova was the Corps' senior non-com, she knew her job was to support the regimental commander. Not that it stopped her telling Ash exactly what she thought when they were alone.

"Instead of sending Lt. Connery—and this isn't knocking her. She's a credit to the Corps, but she's still green as an officer—send Captain Anderson. Not only does she have the reputation of being a no-nonsense Marine, but she knows how you think. If the shit hits the fan, she will know what to do. Besides, doing so will send a message to the Midlothians who are smart enough to check our public bios. It tells them you aren't taking any chances with Nelms."

Ashlyn leaned back and lifted her booted feet onto the corner of her desk. For several long moments, she considered Anismova's suggestion. As she did, she admitted it made sense. M. J. Adamson made a reputation almost as formidable as Anisimova's as a non-com before being mustanged to her current rank. Having the two of them as part of the Secretary's escort should make anyone think twice before trying anything.

But there was another factor, one the sergeant major didn't mention, to consider. Nelms was more likely to listen to a captain than he was a lieutenant. Even so, she wanted Connery to get the experience of dealing with politicians and she knew the chance to serve closely with Anisimova was something she didn't want to take away from the young woman.

"Let's compromise. I'll put MJ in command of the escort team, but I want Connery to go as well." She stopped Anisimova before the woman could interrupt. "Edita, she needs the seasoning as an officer. More than that, I remember my first assignment. Working closely with you, helped me learn how to be an officer. I'm asking you to do the same with her. You can relate to her on a level I can't. She joined the Corps as a private and never expected to be anything but the best non-com she could. Suddenly finding herself wearing bars has thrown her. She's done a damned good job hiding it, but I know her. I've seen the insecurity when she thinks no one is looking."

For a moment, the blonde said nothing. Then she nodded. Seeing how the blonde's eyes twinkled, Ash narrowed her eyes in suspicion. Anisimova was up to something and she knew the woman well enough to realize it didn't bode well for her.

"I think we both know the Midlothians are going to do everything they can to delay our mission. That means Admiral Tremayne and Secretary Nelms will likely order us to evacuate the embassy and other allied holdings in the system. When that happens and when the Midlothians realize we are pulling out, the shit will hit the fan. You need to make sure the regimental elements are ready to not only repel anyone foolish enough to try to board our ships but to carry out SAR dirtside. If that happens, I know you, kid. You're going to want to lead the charge. You can't. You'll be needed up here to coordinate our efforts. Promise me you'll stay here."

Ash frowned. She'd been played and she knew it. Anisimova was right. She would want to lead any SAR mission if things went south. But, as regimental commander, her place wasn't on the front line but behind the scenes, coordinating and making sure her people were getting the orders and support they needed. Damn it, she hated command at times like this.

Still, what were the chances they would face any real challenge from the Midlothians? The government was the sort to work behind the scenes, playing one party against another. They didn't have the stomach for direct action. What harm could come from agreeing to Anisimova's terms?

"Agreed." She laughed softly when Anisimova looked at her in open suspicion.

"That was too easy. What are you planning?"

"For once, I can honestly say nothing." She waited until the sergeant major sighed and nodded once. "Edita, you're right. My place is here, at least in the situation you described. But let's be honest. The Midlothians may bluster and bluff but they won't try anything. In fact, I have a feeling that once they realize we're serious about not only pulling out our corporate and diplomatic personnel and their dependents but our military as well, they'll be begging us to stay. When that happens, they'll do just about anything Nelms asks them to."

"But?"

"I've got a bad feeling about the other factor in this equation."

Anisimova looked as if she understood. "The Callusians?"

Ash nodded. "I know FleetCom feels we have time, possibly weeks or even months, before they strike back over what we did to them in the Savitar VI System. I'm not so sure. We not only managed to free the system, but we defeated one of their most revered commanders. Unlike most people, they won't spend time mourning their losses. They will want vengeance for Dadd's death. Add to that what they see as the Midlothians' betrayal and everything lines up for them setting their sights on this system in the very near future. I want to make sure we're prepared if that happens while we're on-station."

"You and the admiral are of the same mind."

"We've had a few discussions about it." To say the very least. "I'm going to let you in on some of what we've discussed. If things do go south while you're dirtside, there's the very real possibility Nelms will dig his heels in. He'll want to stay until the embassy staff and dependents have been moved onto ships. He'll want to keep negotiating with the government. Neither of those things will happen. Is that understood?" She pinned Anisimova with a look that had the woman nodding in agreement. "I don't care what you have to do, but at the first sign of trouble, he is to be tossed onto a shuttle and removed to safety. That order comes not only from me and Miranda but from President Harper himself."

"I'll make sure of it." She leaned forward, elbows on her knees. As she did, her expression turned serious. "Are you sure about sending us down in full battle rattle?"

Ash arched one brow.

"Okay," the blonde laughed. "It's not really full battle rattle but the pols won't know it. We're likely to scare them to death."

"Good." Ash dropped her feet to the floor and stood. "Edita, I hope they shit themselves when they see you. How many of our people, how many of our friends, have died because of their machinations?" She held up a hand before the blonde could respond. "Too many. But no more. We put an end to it now, one way or another. That's not just my order or Miranda's. It comes straight from the president."

"Can't say I disagree." Anisimova stood and checked her wrist unit. "I'd best go gear up."

"I'll be there with final orders in fifteen." Ash walked with her to the hatch. "Watch yourself down there, Durga."

"I will." She rested a hand on Ash's upper arm. "I'm proud of you, kid, and I'm proud to be serving with you again."

"Same here."

Back at her desk, Ashlyn sat and considered what she wanted to say to the escort team. But first, she needed to tell both Connery and Adamson they would be part of the team. Before she did that, however, she needed to get her worry for Adamson under control. This was the woman's first away mission since nearly losing her life six months earlier. Hopefully, she was right and nothing unforeseen would happen.

---

GOVERNMENT CENTER
*Caspian Bay, Midlothian*

"SECRETARY OF STATE Marc Nelms and Ambassador Morgan Izaguirre." Bethany Waas' aide announced before standing aside so Nelms could enter the conference room. As he did, both Waas and Jensen Vreman stood and turned to the doorway.

"Thank you, Josiah. That will be all." Waas waited until he left before turning her attention to Nelms. "Secretary Nelms, Ambassador Izaguirre, welcome. Please be seated."

The two men settled on one side of the table, opposite Waas and Vreman. Nelms leaned back, folding his hands on the tabletop. As he did, he studied not only the two sitting across from him but the rest of the room. A slight smile touched one corner of his mouth as the door slid open once again and Captain Anderson stepped inside. The Marine didn't speak. Instead, she took up a position to one side of the door. As she did, the message was clear. She, not to mention the five armored Marines in the outer room, were there to keep anything from happening to either him or Izaguirre. From the way both Waas and Vreman looked at her and swallowed hard, they knew it as well.

Good.

"Thank you for meeting with us," Nelms began. "This shouldn't take too long. I believe we can all agree the evidence concerning Alexander Watchman and his machinations with the Callusians is irrefutable. More than that, we can agree not only Fuercon has suffered as a result of their betrayal but so have our allies."

"As we have told the ambassador, the Administrative Bureau is extremely troubled by the evidence. We had no idea Watchman was working with our common enemy," Waas said.

Nelms inclined his head slightly. Let them make of it what they would. As for him, he believed the woman no more than he did any of the other explanations the government sent in response to President Harper's communiques. But he would play the game, at least for a little while.

"I believe Ambassador Izaguirre informed you last week of our government's demands. President Harper sent me to do whatever is necessary to move these negotiations along and bring them to a satis-factory conclusion, one we can all live with."

It wasn't a threat, at least not directly, but his meaning was clear judging from the way Vreman started before getting himself under control.

"I assure you, Secretary Nelms, we have been doing all we can to fulfill those demands," the Chairman said.

"Excellent." He allowed himself a smile that didn't reach his eyes. "Then you have your prisoners and all data your intelligence corps has gathered ready to hand over."

"I'm afraid you are operating under a misunderstanding, Mr. Secretary," Vreman said.

"Really?" Nelms tilted his head to one side, his expression thoughtful. "Are you denying the fact you arrested five members of the Bureau less than a month ago, not to mention others in the government, and charged them with crimes stemming from their association with Alexander Watchman?" He glanced at his datapad and then looked up once again. "I believe those arrested who were removed from the Bureau are Admiral Horace Boniface, Dominic Delespino, Charles Logaine and Sarah Lamar. Also arrested several days later was Katrina Jacoby, among others."

For a long moment, no one spoke. Nelms wasn't sure the Midlothians breathed or their hearts beat. Instead, he watched as the blood drained from their faces. Then they shook off their surprise over the fact he knew what had happened within the presumed sanctity of the government chambers.

"You seem to know a great deal, Mr. Nelms," Vreman said, his voice as cold as ice.

"It pays to know the situation before you step into the arena, Mr. Vreman." Without looking in her direction, he signaled Adamson to stand ready. If the Midlothians tried anything, it would be in the next few moments.

"We have made several arrests, Mr. Secretary." Waas shot a warning look at Vreman before continuing. "However, our intelligence officers are still in the process of questioning them and following up on any and all information they've given us. No one wants to act precipitously on unconfirmed information."

"I assumed no less." Nelms leaned back, giving his best impression of someone relaxed and unconcerned. "When can we tell Admiral Tremayne to expect to have the prisoners transferred to her custody?"

"Mr. Nelms, I assure you, we want to do everything we can to work with you and your government on this," Vreman said. "However, we have our own laws we must follow, and we must determine exactly how deeply the conspiracy runs. Alexander Watchman betrayed more than just Fuercon when he entered into his agreement with the Callusians. As we told Ambassador Izaguirre, it will be up to our courts to determine the exact procedure necessary to turn any of the prisoners over to your government."

"I see." Nelms glanced at Izaguirre and nodded once. The ambassador opened the old-fashioned portfolio he carried. The man made a show of looking inside before withdrawing a sheaf of papers. Nelms accepted them and glanced at them before returning his gaze to the Midlothians. "As suggested, Ambassador Izaguirre presented our case to the Federal Constitution Court. It heard our plea and has granted us custody of the prisoners as well as any evidence seized." He slid a copy of the order across the table and waited as Vreman reached for it.

"However, we want to be reasonable about this. We knew Midlothian interests must be protected. However, do not take our reasonableness for weakness. You have three days to turn the prisoners over to us. I expect you to open the evidence up to our investigators starting immediately.

"I suggest you not try to drag this process out. It would be a serious mistake for you to refuse to turn the prisoners over. As Ambassador Izaguirre informed you earlier, there will serious repercussions to your actions—or inactions. President Harper has issued orders for all Fuerconese and allied dependents to be evacuated to our ships. Captain Middleton is coordinating those efforts with Admiral Tremayne." Nelms stood. "If you refuse to allow us access to all the evidence your seized so far, we will begin withdrawing our diplomatic corps. You have one hour to comply.

"If, at the end of the seventy-two hours, you have failed to turn over the prisoners—and do not doubt we know exactly who has been arrested and why—Admiral Tremayne will withdraw not only our ships but all allied ships from the system."

"We don't take kindly to being threatened, Mr. Secretary." Vreman climbed to his feet, his expression stormy. "You and your government must be reasonable. We need time to review this order and determine if we will comply or appeal. It will take time to gather the evidence and arrange for it to be viewed by your people."

"You have our demands, Mr. Chairman." He motioned to Izaguirre and they moved toward the door. He paused halfway there and turned back. "Do not make the mistake of believing we don't understand exactly how Alexander Watchman was able to do what he did. Your government allowed him to operate without checks and balances because he did your dirty work—and because he has the dirt on too many people in power for his secrets to come to light. You were supposed to be our allies and yet you allowed him to work against not only our best interests but your own as well. Do not make an even graver mistake of believing we will not do as we have said."

With that, he once again turned. He left the room, Izaguirre and Adamson following. As they stepped into the outer room, the rest of the Marine escort fell into place around them. No one spoke until they were safely on their transport and headed back to the embassy.

"Captain, please inform your colonel that it might be wise to increase security around allied embassies. I'll be sending an update to the ambassadors once we're back at the embassy."

"Already done, Mr. Ambassador."

He nodded, impressed. "Morgan, let Captain Middleton know there is no change in his orders. Let's get all but essential personnel off-planet. The Midlothians need to see we're serious about this and aren't going to back down."

He doubted Vreman would try anything, but he wasn't going to take any risks. He'd drawn a line in the sand, so to speak. The next move was up to the Midlothians and he prayed they did nothing foolish.

# 11

*ATLANTIS RISING, FLAGSHIP*
*First Fleet, Fuerconese Navy*
*Midlothian space*

"WELL, WHAT DO YOU THINK?"

Miranda Tremayne glanced at the three gathered in her office. Captain Raoul Kohler had just come off duty and looked more than ready to find his bed. Secretary Nelms looked equally as tired, not that it surprised her. In the two days since their arrival in-system, he had been in lengthy negotiations with the Midlothians. But it was Ashlyn Shaw who drew her attention. The younger woman looked tired but there was something else about her, something Tremayne recognized. Ash was worried. Trusting her Marine commander's instincts, the admiral made a quick mental note to find out why.

"They're still trying to play us," Nelms said. He nodded in appreciation as Tremayne handed him a mug of coffee. "But Waas is finally beginning to understand President Harper and the rest of the allies are determined to see this through."

"And Vreman?" she asked as she offered Ash a mug.

"He's still holding out. My take on it is he will give in but only at the last minute. He's walking a very fine line right now. He needs to find a way to regain the trust of the rest of the government, not to mention the voters, but he also has to make sure we don't pull our military support. Add in a healthy dose of fear about what Watchman's files will reveal if we find them before his side does and he is a man being pulled in a number of different directions."

"Will he acquiesce before the deadline?" Captain Kohler asked.

Nelms shrugged. "That I don't know. That's why I've instructed Ambassador Izaguirre to continue the withdrawal of our people. President Harper was very clear before we left the home system. If the Midlothians don't do as we've asked, we will leave them to their own devices. It is time for those who have taken advantage of our protection to understand we won't stand by and let them use us and betray us all at the same time."

"If I may?" Ash placed her mug on the table to her right and leaned forward, elbows on her knees. When Tremayne nodded, she continued. "We started seeing a change in attitude from the Midlothians, especially from the general populace, late yesterday when they noticed that not only were our people withdrawing from the surface but so are our allies. Captain Kohler will know the numbers better than I do but our shuttles have been running non-stop as they evacuate non-essential personnel and dependents. I want to commend Captain Middleton and Ambassador Izaguirre for anticipating Secretary Nelms' orders and starting the evacuation before we arrived."

Nelms nodded in agreement. "Thank you, Colonel. I'll make sure to pass on your comments."

"What do you suggest our next step be?" Tremayne asked.

Kohler drained his mug and set it on the floor next to his left boot. "We continue as we have been. If the shit hits the fan, I want everyone onboard. The last thing we need is to have a bunch of shuttles out of service because they are either still ferrying people up from the surface or because they haven't been battle prepped."

Tremayne glanced at Ash and noted how she winced slightly when Kohler mentioned the shuttles being caught ferrying people up from the surface. Not that she blamed the young woman. The wound left by the deaths of Talbot and the others on the shuttle with him would take time to heal.

"Mr. Secretary?"

"I agree. We must hold firm and not deviate from our orders. If the Midlothians fail to turn over the prisoners within the time limit, we withdraw from the system. However, I would recommend we hold the fleet close enough to respond should the Callusians decide this is a good time to strike."

Tremayne leaned back and considered his suggestion. Her orders left her some leeway, especially if she felt the system was in danger. Angry as everyone was with Watchman's betrayal and the way the government looked the other way, no one in the government or military wanted to sacrifice a system of innocents just to punish a few politicians.

"What have we learned from the data they've turned over so far?" she asked.

"Let's just say they are being very careful about not only what they turn over to us but in what order they do so," Nelms said.

Tremayne frowned and listened as he continued. She knew the Midlothian government had done its best to drag out the process, initially refusing to allow Major Khan and his team access to the original data seized from Watchman's office and other holdings. That changed quickly when Khan contacted both Nelms and Ashlyn. Nelms had a "discussion" with Waas about the situation while Ash took more direct action. She ordered a squad of Devil Dogs under Anisimova's command to report to Khan. Major Khan then stood aside and let the sergeant major have a short "discussion" with the Midlothian intelligence officer preventing them from doing their jobs. Khan reported Anisimova very quickly put the man in his place and he swore he saw a tear in the Midlothian's eye. Even so, the data exchange had taken longer than it should.

But Khan and his people were finding some interesting tidbits in what data had been turned over. Unfortunately, the main question they all had remained unanswered. They still didn't know where Watchman was.

"Have they given us access to Watchman's holdings and the rest of the data?" Captain Kohler asked.

Nelms shook his head, his expression sour. "Not yet. I've already discussed the situation with Colonel Shaw and we're going to make a *statement* the next time we go groundside."

"Oh?" Tremayne glanced from Nelms to Ash, her mouth thinning when the younger woman refused to look at her. She had a feeling she wasn't going to like hat they had in mind.

"I'll be accompanying Secretary Nelms and his escort today, ma'am," Ash said. "Captain Anderson will be in command here. Lt. Connery will remain as well to assist. But Sergeant Major Anisimova will be part of the escort team. I have a feeling that, between the two of us, we might be able to impress upon the Midlothians how important it is they cooperate."

Tremayne pictured the scene and nodded. Unless the Midlothians were complete fools, they knew Ashlyn's history. They knew she would do whatever it took to defeat the Callusians and that she had little use for anyone aiding the enemy. Her presence might do the trick. But did they dare risk her on the mission? If something happened, she would be needed on the flag ship to help coordinate the Marines during battle.

"All right." She pinned Ash with a firm look. "But if I order you back to the fleet, no matter what the excuse, you are to obey without question and without delay. Understood?"

"Understood, ma'am."

The young woman might have said the right thing but the rebellious flash in her eyes told Tremayne she didn't appreciate the order. Too bad. She wasn't going to be the one to tell Elizabeth Shaw her eldest child wasn't going to return from the mission.

"Let's move on," Tremayne said. "Any other questions?"

"What about the new defense platforms?" Ashlyn asked.

"They will be moved into place today. We'll keep them, as well as the sensor arrays, powered down to passive status for now. Controls are tied directly to this ship with secondary control linked to Captain Middleton's ship." Tremayne considered for a moment before continuing. "It's no secret that we're taking a book out of Admiral Collins' book here. We're not letting the government know what we're doing. However, since they might have learned what was done in the Savitar VI System and might conclude we would try the same thing here, the techs have masked the passive signals. FleetCom wants to make sure anyone still working with Watchman in unable to warn him or the Callusians about our safeguards."

"Vreman won't like it when he finds out." Nelms sounded almost gleeful and Tremayne looked at him in surprise. "He likes to think he's the one in charge of the Bureau but I'm starting to believe the real power lies with Waas. She is not only very capable, but I have a feeling she is the one working behind the scenes, making sure things get done."

"Captain Adamson happens to agree with you, sir," Ash said. "She's been taking careful note of the Midlothians when she's been part of your escort. Her observations basically come down to Vreman doesn't mind taking the hard road if it protects his interests which, at least at the moment, means Midlothian's best interests. Waas, on the other hand, is the one who seems to see the whole picture."

"Colonel Shaw's correct. There have been times when I've said or done something they didn't expect. Each time, it's been Waas to make the initial response with Vreman following up."

"What do we know about her?" Tremayne asked.

"Not much and that is a point of concern." Nelms rubbed his chin. "I've asked Major Khan to get me a full dossier on her."

Their conversation stopped as Tremayne's comm beeped softly, signaling an incoming call. She reached up and touched her earbud and listened, a smile slowly spreading across her face. She thanked the comms officer and turned her attention back to the others.

"It seems the Midlothians have decided to relent at least a little. They'll be transferring the prisoners to our custody by end of day."

"Then, if you will excuse me, Admiral, I'd like to confer with Major

Khan and then Ambassador Izaguirre. There will be some arrangements to be made." Nelms climbed to his feet.

"Of course, Mr. Secretary. I'd appreciate it if we could meet before you head back down to the planet."

"Give me an hour or so, Admiral."

She nodded and waited for him to leave. Then she turned her attention to the others. "Captain Koehler, go get some rest. I'll bring you up to speed later."

"Thank you, ma'am."

"Now, Ash," she continued once they were alone. "Have you discussed your plans with Anisimova?" She had no doubt the blonde would tell Ash if she thought the idea was a bad one.

"I have and she agreed with me. MJ was the one I had to convince."

"Let me guess. She wanted you to remain up here and leave the detail to her."

Ash nodded. "Part of it is because she needs to prove to herself that she has recovered as much from her injuries as we know she has. Part of it is her need to protect me. She lost Lucinda on her watch, even though she was already injured badly enough she was out of action. Whether she admits it or not, she wants to do everything she can to make sure nothing happens to me."

"Just as you want to make sure nothing else happens to her." Tremayne understood both of their concerns. "If it makes you feel better, I agree that you are the right person for the escort at this time. We need to shake the Midlothians up some. Your presence should throw them off their game." She hoped. "But I meant it, Ash. If I order you back to the ship, you aren't to hesitate. You're to get your ass on a shuttle and get up here."

"I understand, Miranda."

And, judging by her expression, she did. Realizing it, Tremayne relaxed. "Are you getting any pushback from the Navy side on anything?"

Ash grimaced slightly and shrugged. "You know how it is. There are still some who feel Marines shouldn't be anything more than boots on the ground fighters. I know you've done your best to weed those who feel that way out of the fleet but there are a few who don't agree with my people backing their specialists up."

Tremayne frowned. She thought that old argument would have been put to bed by Ashlyn herself. It hadn't been that long ago the younger woman had to take command of one of the ships in Tremayne's command when the captain was injured in battle. Ash had done a better job than many naval officers would have in that situation.

"Who?"

Ash shook her head and Tremayne bit back a sigh. "Let MJ and I deal with it. We've set up some sims for those ships involved to run, sims that will take ship commanders out of action and then cut off AuxCon. Let's see what happens."

"All right." She intended to observe the sims and see first-hand how both the Marines and their naval counterparts responded.

Ash checked her wrist unit and stood. "If you'll excuse me, I need to brief MJ and Connery."

"Go. But not unnecessary risks, Ash. I mean it."

"Heard and understood, ma'am." She grinned and Tremayne shook her head.

"Keep your comms open once you hit the surface."

"Yes, Mom," she drawled with a cheeky grin.

"Get out of here." Tremayne laughed. "But be ready to join me for dinner after you return."

"Yes, ma'am."

Ash threw a half-salute and left. As the hatch slid shut behind her, Tremayne blew out a long breath. Even though things were going much as she expected, she couldn't shake the feeling this was the calm before the storm. If she was right, she needed to make sure the fleet was ready for the proverbial shoe to drop.

# 1 2

---

"COLONEL."

Ashlyn didn't wince but it was a close thing. She knew that tone of voice. Her aide was not happy. Nor, judging by the look on M. J. Adamson's face, was her executive officer. Wondering what was wrong, Ash finished putting away her weapons before straightening to face the music. As she did, she felt a bit like a teen caught sneaking back in after missing curfew.

"What's happened?" she asked simply as she began stripping out of her armor.

Lt. Faith Connery stepped up to help. As she did, the young woman looked in Adamson's direction. Seeing it, Ash frowned slightly. They were up to something and she didn't have a clue what.

"Ma'am, we've had news from home." Adamson's voice might have been bland, but her expression was thunderous.

Not liking the fact neither volunteered any more, she finished removing her armor and quickly dressed. Then she sat on the long bench in front of the lockers and reached for her boots.

"Tell me."

She braced herself. Their grim demeanor could mean any number of things, none of them good. None of them things she wanted to think about, not here, so far from where she could do anything about whatever the problem might be.

"We don't know the full details," Anderson said. "The message said further details and amended orders would be forthcoming."

"Just say it, MJ."

"The enemy struck again. This time in the Bennington System. They attempted to use the biotoxin against the capital planet."

Ash felt the blood drain from her face, and she swallowed hard. Then she realized what her XO said. "Attempted?"

Both women nodded. "The missiles were intercepted. Several LACs sacrificed themselves to intercept the missiles. But we also lost the *Sullivan* and the *Kamura*."

"What aren't you telling me?"

And why wouldn't they get to it?

"Both ships were hit with missiles loaded with the biotoxin." Adamson's voice was soft, almost anguished.

Ash closed her eyes and offered up a quick prayer for the dead. "Where did you get the intel from?"

"Your mother. She said further info will come as soon as they have it."

Ash nodded and thought hard. This was exactly what she'd tried warning the brass about. It didn't matter her mother and Okafor agreed with her. FleetCom believed they had more time. Had that cost all those souls their lives?

"Where's the admiral?" Ash knew her mother would have sent word to Tremayne, hopefully with more detail.

"In her quarters," Connery said. "She left orders for you to report there as soon as you returned to the ship."

"All right." She rubbed her hands over her face. "Brief Edita. Unless I miss my guess, Okafor will have sent her an update. See if she knows anything more than we do. Start pulling together not only amended training schedules, focusing on the new protocols, but also updated OOB based on what we know so far about what happened in the Bennington System."

Standing, she made up her mind. "Until we know more, let's reinforce Nelms' security team as well as embassy security. Put our LACs on standby. Make sure our people understand I will have the heads of anyone not following every part of the new protocols concerning the biotoxin. I do not want to lose anyone to carelessness or stupidity. Understood?"

"Understood," they both said.

"I'll comm when I leave the admiral's quarters."

As she made her way through the ship to Tremayne's quarters, she noted the change in atmosphere. Even though official word might not have come about what happened in the Bennington System, unofficial word had leaked out. There was a grimness to the crew that hadn't been there when she left the ship six hours earlier. Along with the grimness was a determination she recognized and shared. Every member of the crew, be they Navy or Marine, wanted to avenge the latest attack. As far as Ash was concerned, that couldn't come too soon.

"You heard," Tremayne said as she motioned Ash inside a short time later.

"MJ and Faith were waiting for me when I returned to the ship." She nodded in appreciation when Tremayne handed her a beer. "They didn't know much, just the bare bones." She left the question unasked, trusting Tremayne to tell her what she knew.

"Let's sit." The admiral indicated the sitting area across the room. Ash followed and settled onto one of the chairs. "What did they say?"

"Like I said, they didn't know much. The Callusians attacked the Bennington System. Some of our LAC pilots sacrificed themselves to intercept missiles loaded with the biotoxin. Despite that and despite the best efforts of the other ships on-station, we still lost the *Sullivan* and the *Kamura* to that damned biotoxin." She took a long pull on her beer.

"That's the short version and pretty much what FleetCom's forwarded to me." Tremayne leaned back and crossed her ankles. "Reading between the lines, the enemy transitioned in-system without warning and immediately open fired. The *Sullivan* was lost because a missile carrying the biotoxin hit Engineering. Between the damage to the section and the loss of all hands stationed there, the engines went critical and the ship exploded. The only good thing that happened was the captain managed to get almost half the crew into life pods before systems went critical. Because he followed protocol, the biotoxin was confined to Engineering and one hangar bay. None of those who escaped were exposed."

Ash nodded, relieved to know the new protocol appeared to work. "And the *Kamura*?"

"The CO fucked up. There's no other way to say it." Anger roughened Tremayne's voice and Ash frowned. It was rare for the woman to let her emotion show in this kind of a situation.

"Miranda?"

"He didn't follow the new protocols. Two missiles loaded with the biotoxin made it through the ship's defenses. Under most circumstances, the ship would have survived the strikes. But by the time he realized what happened and ordered the new protocols put into place, the biotoxin had gotten into the environmental systems. His crew was doomed."

Ash cursed softly. No wonder Tremayne was angry. Negligence caused the deaths of so many good men and women. Damn it!

"Captain Burnam prepared his log and then downloaded it as well as the ship's logs to the *Charon*. Then he set a collision course with the enemy flag ship. That turned the battle and the squadron was able to not only turn aside the attack but hold the system. Reinforcements are already headed there."

Ash frowned and set her beer down on the table between their chairs. Then she stood. She needed to move, to pace. Otherwise, she might just explode. This was exactly the sort of strike she'd feared from the enemy. They'd gotten lucky—if you could call it luck that they lost only two ships and who knew how many LACs. Maybe now FleetCom would realize how foolish it was for First Fleet, not to mention 10$^{th}$Div7$^{th}$ Reg, to be parked and out of the action.

"Have we gotten updated orders?"

"Not yet. At least not officially." She frowned and Ash guessed she liked being left out of the fighting no more than she did. "Unofficially, we are to finish up here as quickly as possible and head back to the home system. Once we off-load non-military personnel and any data and/or prisoners, we will be shipping out to join the main push."

"Finally." It couldn't happen too soon. "Have you briefed Nelms?"

"Not yet. I wanted the two of us to put our heads together and run various scenarios before I did."

Ash nodded and finished her beer. After setting her bottle to one side, she turned and paced the length of the sitting room. As she did, she wondered if the Bennington System attack was the shoe she'd been waiting to drop or just the prelude to something much worse.

"Miranda, have there been any other attacks?" she asked as she turned back to face the woman.

The admiral shook her head. "No, and that bothers me. The Callusians have never limited themselves to one sector of battle."

"That worries me as well. Unfortunately, there are a number of possible targets they could be closing in on as we speak."

"Including here," Tremayne said.

Ash nodded.

"Suggestions?"

Ash didn't answer immediately. Instead she considered the various options. Part of her wanted to say the fleet needed to withdraw from the system and leave the Midlothians to fend for themselves. She pushed the thought back. FleetCom was right. They couldn't leave the system unprotected. But they also couldn't sit there, waiting. At least not for long.

"Honestly?" she asked and Tremayne nodded. "We implement the new compartment protocol immediately." She shook her head when the admiral opened her mouth to say something. "Miranda, I know your ship commanders have everything in place to lock it down at the first sign of trouble. But so, supposedly, did the *Sullivan* and *Kamura*. Unfortunately for their crews, the enemy got the drop on them. We can't risk that happening here."

Tremayne frowned and nodded in agreement. "What else?"

"Keep the new defense platforms and sensor arrays on passive but move them into position to cover any gaps in the current array system." Ashlyn paused, considering what else. "Nelms needs to quit playing politics with the Midlothians. He either gets the last of the information they are holding back or we pull the rest of our people off-planet and withdraw our ships."

"And your Marines?"

"I've already issued orders putting my Marines on full alert status. LAC and attack shuttle crews are to bunk hot in the hangars. The birds are to be kept flight prepped. We're increasing the number of escorts for both Nelms and the Major Khan's people. They will be in full battle rattle and are to let me know if the Midlothians give them any grief over it."

"As soon as we finish here, issue orders to all fleet Marines to do the same. Let's not take any risks with your people. They will be the first line of defense going forward, especially for Nelms and his people, not to mention those of our people still on-planet."

"Understood." She thought for a moment. "Miranda, I got the impression during today's negotiations that at least one member of the Bureau knows where Watchman is. Either that or they know how to get into contact with him. I recommend Nelms and Izaguirre confront him with any evidence to support my hunch that Khan's people have managed to pull together. I can't help feeling that if we don't grab up Watchman now, we'll never get him."

Tremayne sat back and looked at her thoughtfully. "You think he's still on the planet?"

Ash understood the admiral's reaction. They'd had their suspicions since their arrival in-system. In fact, the more then Midlothians assured them there was no way the former Intelligence Czar was on the planet, the more convinced they became that he was. Ash lost all doubt during the day's negotiations. Today she'd changed not only the makeup of the Secretary of State's escort but her role as well. Instead of standing guard at the door as Anderson had when she commanded the escort, Ash took her place behind the man as he sat at the table while Anisimova guarded the door. That gave Ashlyn ample opportunity to study each person present. One in particular set off all her internal alarms. Watching him, she noted his reaction every time someone mentioned Watchman's name. He definitely knew more than he let on and it was time to find out what.

"I'll speak to Nelms about it." Now it was Tremayne's turn to fall silent for a few moments. "I want you and Anisimova with him when he returns to the surface, assuming you are confident leaving the ship. But the same restrictions apply as tomorrow as did today. You are to return at the first sign of trouble or if I tell you to. But I want the two of you, along with the biggest, meanest looking Devil Dogs you have, to act as Nelms' escort. Put the fear of God into those damned politicians dirtside. It's time to stop playing games."

"Understood and agree." She returned to her chair. "Miranda, if we're doing this right, we need to be in full battle rattle. Full armor, helmets and faceplates, weaponed up, battlenet active. Also, I'll not be part of the escort party. Nelms will formally introduce to me in my role as the Marine CO of the mission. Unless either you or he have strong objections, I plan to make it very clear to the Administrative Bureau that we will no longer sit still and wait for them to comply with our demands. My duty as Marine CO is simple. My Marines and I will either assist their people in taking Watchman into custody or we will escort Nelms and Izaguirre back to the embassy. From there, we will evacuate them and our people to our ships. That means you have to make sure Nelms agrees with our plan."

"Trust me, I'll make sure he not only knows what you plan but fully supports it." She paused and cocked her head to one side in a manner that told Ash she was listening to a comm. "It seems we both have new messages coming in from FleetCom. I suggest you see what your mother has to say and then be prepared for a briefing. Lt. Meyer will inform you of the time."

"Yes, ma'am." She stood. "Miranda, we're heading toward the endgame. I feel it. I just wish I felt more confident about the outcome."

"I know, Ash. The biotoxin and what it can do has thrown us all off our game. But we have an effective if inconvenient workaround. Remember that."

"I'll try to." She started for the hatch and then stopped, looking over her shoulder. "Miranda, I recommend all essential personnel be in light armor going forward. Let's not get caught with our pants around our ankles."

"Let me think about it."

Ash frowned slightly but didn't argue. She'd bring the recommendation back up during the briefing. If the Callusians did attempt to launch a sneak attack on the system, they needed to be prepared and not scrambling to secure essential areas of the ship or essential personnel. Hell, the admiral was lucky she hadn't recommended all personnel go to full battle gear all the time.

"Miranda, we both know the enemy is going to target this system. The only question is when. You've already taken steps to prevent them from being successful. Don't let yourself get overconfident now. Please." She turned to fully look at the woman. "You're protecting the crew. You're protecting those loyal to Fuercon and our allies on the surface. Do me a favor and protect yourself as well."

"I promise to think about everything you've said." She moved to stand before Ash and rested a hand on her arm. "But you need to take your own advice. I want you taking precautions, you and all your Marines."

"Trust me, we will." Even if she had to kick every Marine butt to see to it. "Do you want Adamson or Anisimova at the briefing?"

"Both. Connery as well."

"I'll make sure they know."

With that, she left the admiral's quarters. As she did, she had a feeling it was going to be a very long night.

---

ASH SETTLED behind her desk and reached for her mug. She'd prefer a large whiskey but knew better. She needed a clear mind, not only to listen to the message from General Okafor that just arrived, as well as one from her mother, but to brief her senior officers. If she managed an hour's sack time before transporting down to the surface, she'd be lucky.

She punched in a command and leaned back, blowing across the top of her mug. A moment later, Helen Okafor's image appeared on her screen. The general looked as grim as Ashlyn felt. That wasn't good, not good at all.

"Colonel Shaw, there are developments you need to know about," Okafor said without preamble. "I'm aware your mother sent you a basic brief. Since then, more information has come to light, information you need to be aware of. There is also a change in your orders.

"One week ago, an element of Fifth Fleet was attacked while on station in the Bennington System. Enemy ships translated into the system without warning and caught our ships unprepared." She went on to confirm everything Elizabeth and later Tremayne had told Ash.

"Colonel, we managed to turn back the enemy but not without great cost. That cost, however, confirmed our fears. The enemy has managed to produce enough of the biotoxin to use it with at least some of their missiles. This information means naval tactics must be adapted. FleetCom is already working on that and will be sending updated orders and recommendations to Admiral Tremayne in very short order.

"As for your Marines, new orders are as follows. First, daily sims are to be run. They are to be split between holo and live action. In both, the Marines are to be armored up. Standard warfare simulations combined with those where the biotoxin is used. Make sure your people respond automatically with the new protocols. Let's not lose any more Marines to this damned biotoxin.

"Second, any time a Marine is on duty outside of the home system and certain allied systems, which will be laid out in the memo following this message, they are to be in light armor if onboard a ship or medium to heavy armor, depending on his specialty, if part of a landing party.

"Third, I have been informed by FleetCom and by President Harper that the timeframe for your current mission has been cut. If the Midlothian Administrative Bureau has not met our demands within the next forty-eight hours, First Fleet is to pull out of the system and return home. It is my understanding that FleetCom will authorize Admiral Tremayne to leave the sensor arrays and defense platforms she launched to help cover the system. However, the fleet is not to delay its departure any longer than that.

"From now until your regiment returns to Fuercon, you are now in command of not only the regiment but of those Marines assigned to Captain Middleton's command. All appropriate orders have been sent to Captain Middleton as the naval commander and to Major Bischoff, Marine CO. Integrate them into the regiment the best you can in the short time you have. Make sure they are as comfortable with the new protocols as your Marines are."

Okafor paused and from the way she looked to her right, Ashlyn guessed someone had come into her office. When she turned back to the screen, Okafor looked, if possible, even more concerned.

"Ash, we just received confirmation of another Callusian attack. This time they struck Goran's Rest. The station was destroyed. If there is any good news, it is that initial reports do not indicate the biotoxin was used."

Ash cursed and brought up an astro map on her data pad. Goran's Rest was on a line that ran from the Bennington System to Midlothian space. If that wasn't enough to worry her, the fact the way station was owned by Midlothian was. The Callusians' message was clear: they could destroy Midlothian's holdings and they could destroy the home system. The only question was when.

"By the time you get this message, the Callusians very well may be knocking on your door. Do not take any chances. You are one of my best Marines and those you command are a credit to you and to the Corps. Your primary duty right now is to protect our people. Secretary of State Nelms is not to fall into enemy hands. Nor is Admiral Tremayne. If you have to knock both of them out and confine them to quarters to make sure they are kept safe, do it. Get them and yourself home safe. This fight just got real and we're going to need your regiment to help bring this war to an end.

"A full explanation of your orders is included with this message. I will be in contact as more information comes available. Okafor out."

The image changed to the regiment's wallpaper and Ash leaned back. She didn't like the idea of leaving the system open to invasion.

But if it came down to choosing between protecting Midlothian space or her home system or even taking the battle to the Callusians, the answer was clear. Fuercon had to be protected and if going after the Callusians meant an end to the war, it was worth the risk. The blame for the current situation didn't lie with FleetCom or General Okafor. Nor did it lie with Fuercon's government. No, it lay firmly at the feet of Alexander Watchman and the Midlothian government.

She leaned forward and activated her comm. "Faith, send for MJ and Edita. Then ask the mess to send up coffee and sandwiches. We've received new orders and it looks like we have a long night ahead of us," she said over the comm.

"Understood, Colonel."

Ash reached for her datapad and scanned the orders Okafor sent with her message. The war had taken an unexpected turn with the events on Shennong. Fuercon and her allies were still trying to catch up. The Callusians had upped the stakes and she prayed her Marines were up to the task. It was up to her to make sure they were.

# 13

---

Alexander Watchman ended the comm and frowned. He'd made the decision long before it became necessary to disappear from public view not to abandon Midlothian. It didn't matter his government had abandoned him, at least for the moment. All that mattered was making sure the mission was ultimately successful. If it was, Midlothian would finally assume its rights place of prominence among the major powers in the sector. If not, well, there wouldn't be anything left for them to worry about. The Callusians would see to that.

Unfortunately, he hadn't planned on Derek Harper and his administration. Under Harper's leadership, Fuercon became a threat instead of the ally he'd carefully cultivated during the previous administrations. Harper had nothing he could use to *influence* his actions. Worse, the man was being true to his campaign promises of protecting Fuercon and her allies and being victorious over the Callusians.

Then there were the thrice-damned Callusians. They refused to follow his recommendations of moving slowly and not directly confronting Fuercon. That was bad enough. But the use of the biotoxin on Shennong had rallied even the most hesitant of Fuercon's allies behind the battle flag.

And Midlothian was caught right in the middle.

Damn it, how had it all gone so wrong so quickly?

The former Intelligence Czar moved to the rickety desk across the room. The expensive and secure data unit sitting there was in direct conflict with the rest of the room. The flophouse he currently lived in was the perfect hiding place. The other occupants kept them heads down and their eyes and ears closed. No one who knew him before he disappeared would ever consider the possibility of him living in such squalor. All he had to do was survive a little bit longer. Then he'd be able to return to the life he'd left behind.

Assuming the Callusians and the Fuerconese didn't ruin his plans any more than they already had.

And that now seemed like it might be a very real possibility.

At least it was if he were to believe Santos Reyes.

Perhaps he should have left the system when he had the chance. He'd certainly left enough clues behind to make it seem like he had. But he couldn't walk away from everything he'd worked so hard to build over the years. More than that, if he left the system, he placed himself in a position where he couldn't monitor what happened and couldn't apply pressure where needed to continue his mission.

He once again produced his comm and punched in a code. Then he waited, knowing the person on the other end would answer only if it was safe to do so.

"Yes?" a woman's voice said a few moments later. As with all their previous contacts, there was no video. It protected them both by revealing nothing about where either of them happened to be during the calls.

"Reyes commed. Is the situation as bad as he said?"

Silence. Watchman waited, picturing the woman as she decided how to respond.

"It's not good." Another pause. "The pressure is on to reveal anything and everything the Bureau knows, either collectively or individually, about a certain person's whereabouts and activities. Vreman is doing his best to hold out but the Fueronese hold all the cards right now. He won't risk them withdrawing their military support. Not after seeing what the biotoxin can do."

"I assume you are doing all you can to keep the situation in hand."

"Of course. I know who really holds the power here."

He allowed himself a small smile. She did know. Just as she knew what would happen if the information he had on her should find its way into certain people's hands. The best she could hope for was prison. In reality, she'd be lucky to escape with her life. Certain parts of their society didn't take kindly to having their secrets revealed and he would make very certain all trace of betrayal led directly to her.

"How much time do we have?"

"A day, two at most."

Which meant he needed to act fast if he was to stay one step ahead of the Fueronese.

"All right. You've done well."

With that, he ended the comm. Where Reyes tended to overreact and panic, she kept her head. That's what made her such a good tool. Their relationship began years earlier when he discovered some of her clandestine activities and used them to get her cooperation on certain matters before the Bureau. Now she was as close to an ally as he had. Not that he trusted her to keep his secrets without the sword he held over her. Even so, they had formed a relationship that worked for both of them.

That left him with Vreman to consider. The man's dedication to Midlothian couldn't be questioned. Unfortunately, he lacked the backbone necessary to push their system into the leadership position it deserved. Steps needed to be taken to prevent him from caving in to the Fueronese and setting back everything Watchman and the others accomplished.

An hour later, an elderly man dressed in clothes that had seen their better day long ago shuffled through the mass of pedestrians making their way toward the government complex in the center of town. A few feet ahead of him, his target waited at the curb. A member of the security service stood nearby. The agent said something and Jensen Vreman nodded. Then he stepped forward, the crowd surging into the intersection with him.

Watchman slipped between the men and women making their way to their offices. Many of them knew him but none recognized him. Instead, they saw a feeble old man who presented a danger to no one. How little they knew and how foolish they were. Especially Vreman.

"Easy, Chairman," he whispered as he stepped up next to the man. "Listen closely. You know what I'm capable of. Unless you want something to happen to that lovely wife of yours or your equally lovely daughter, you will not sell out to Fuercon. You will send them off with what you've already turned over to them. As far as you're concerned, I left the system weeks ago and you have no idea where I went. As far as you know, I'm dead and you hope I stay that way."

He slipped back into the mass of humanity streaming down the street and was gone before Vreman turned, fear draining the blood from the man's face.

Hopefully, that would be enough to keep him safe until the Fuerconese left the system. It had to be. Vreman and the others knew he wouldn't hesitate to let the streets run red with the blood of his enemies. Now it was time to get to safety.

And the waiting game continued.

# 14

The moment he entered the conference room, Secretary of State Marc Nelms knew something had changed. In his previous discussions with the Administrative Bureau or its representatives, he'd learned who objected to doing anything Fuercon asked, no matter how reasonable or how badly Midlothian needed the continued protection of Fuercon and her allies. Not once during those sessions had he seen Jensen Vreman be anything but open to discussion. Yet, this morning, the man sat at the head of the conference table, his expression set in stone.

Without breaking stride, Nelms signaled his companions to be wary. Not that their Midlothian counterparts realized it. After all, who would be suspicious of him reaching up to scratch his chin? To their credit, none of those accompanying him visibly reacted. Even so, he all but felt Ashlyn Shaw tensing behind him.

He stopped at the far end of the conference table, standing behind the chair he'd occupied every other time he'd been planetside. Ambassador Morgan Izaguirre took his place to Nelms' right. This time, instead of assuming her place by the doorway or at the table, Colonel Shaw moved to stand behind and slightly to the left of his chair. Nelms bent his head to hide his smile as several of those gathered stiffened in response. Obviously, they didn't appreciate having an armed and armored Marine so close.

Too bad. They were about to learn the time for games was over.

"Mr. Secretary, I must object to the colonel's presence and to your obvious attempt to intimidate this body into doing as you wish," Vreman said.

For a moment, Nelms remained silent. Then he pushed his chair back and stood. Izaguirre immediately followed suit. While he hadn't expected the Midlothians to escalate the situation so quickly, he'd been prepared for the possibility.

"I assure you, Chairman, this is not an attempt at intimidation. If it were, you'd know it." He tried hard not to smile when Shaw chuckled almost evilly. Even though he didn't turn, he imagined she was lightly caressing the sidearm at her right thigh, driving home his point for him. "I came bearing a warning, not about what my government might do if you continue to drag your feet and refuse to fulfill the agreements and treaties you signed with Fuercon and our other allies. Instead, I came with a warning about recent activity by our common enemy. However, since you aren't interested in hearing what I have to say, I will take my leave and instruct Admiral Tremayne to finish evacuating our personnel and their dependents to her ships. It is obvious these negotiations have broken down. Good day, ladies and gentlemen. I assure you we will be out of your system within the next twelve hours."

He stepped away from the table. As he did, he nodded once and Colonel Shaw moved to the right, letting him pass. Then she fell in behind him and Izaguirre. He knew without looking, she walked backward toward the door, never taking her attention from the Bureau members. It was a carefully choreographed move, one they'd discussed on the shuttle after they left the *Atlantis Rising*.

Voices murmured behind them. Some concerned, others affronted. All surprised he'd walked away from the table.

"Wait!" Vreman said.

Nelms stopped and turned. "Yes?"

"What warning?"

"Does this mean the Bureau will live up to its agreements with Fuercon?" Izaguirre asked. "We have no desire to continue with the one-way relationship our systems have *enjoyed* these last years." His disgust with the Bureau and its members hung thick in the air.

"We have done all you asked," Bethany Waal said. "It is your government that continues to make ever-increasing impossible demands."

"Then the answer to my question is no." Nelms shook his head, his expression cold. "I will tell you this. Your former allies, the Callusians, have struck at least twice more since the attack on Shennong. Each attack brings them closer to this system. I would suggest warning your citizens so they have time to either put their affairs in order or hopefully get out of the system before it is too late." He glanced at Shaw. "Colonel, please inform the admiral we are on our way back and it is my recommendation we leave the system as soon as possible."

"Yes, sir." She reached up and lightly tapped her earbud, activating her comm.

"Wait!" Everyone in the room heard the panic in Vreman's voice this time. "You can't pull out now."

"Begging the Chairman's pardon, but that is exactly what we can do," Shaw said. For the first time since their arrival, she stepped forward, making herself part of the discussion.

"For those who don't recognize her, let me introduce Colonel Ashlyn Shaw, commanding officer of Tenth Division Seventh Regiment Fuerconese Marine Corps. Colonel Shaw and her command are often on the leading edges of our battle against the Callusians. In fact, the colonel and members of her command returned from Shennong not long before being tasked with this mission. This is just part of the assistance you have refused for your system. This is the help you have refused by continuing to impede our attempts to locate and arrest Alexander Watchman. This is the help you do not have the right to demand now, when you fear for your cowardly lives." Nelms spoke coldly.

"B-but," Waal stammered.

"What do you want?" Vreman slumped in his chair, defeated.

"Exactly what you agreed to give us—Alexander Watchman."

"You'd hold our system hostage just so you can get your revenge on one man?" Santos Reyes demanded.

Nelms' upper lip curled in disgust. "If we wanted revenge, we would have pulled our forces out of the system long ago. What we want is justice. What we require is knowledge of just how far this conspiracy runs. Fuercon and her allies, those who have fought the enemy at our side, have lost millions of lives in this war. Many of those can be laid directly at the feet of Watchman and every person who aided him or turned a blind eye to what he was doing.

"Midlothian claims to be our ally. It's time to prove it." He glanced around the table. "You have one hour to make up your minds. While you do, I will make sure our efforts to get our people to safety continue. Good day."

Nelms once again turned. Ignoring the pleas for him to stay, to negotiate some more, he left the room, Shaw and Izaguirre on his heels.

"We will wait at the embassy," he said as they stepped into their waiting transport a few minutes later. "Colonel, I trust you've improved security there in ways you've not told us about."

Ash nodded once. One of the first things she did when they arrived in-system was dispatch teams to improve security in and around the embassy.

"Then put it all in effect. Let's not take any chances."

"Already done, sir."

"Thank you." He blew out a breath and ran a hand over his face. "I don't want to leave this system unprotected. Not only am I unwilling to sacrifice the citizens who had nothing to do with the machinations of some of those in government, but it would be a PR nightmare for the allies if we did. But that doesn't mean I have any qualms about putting the fear of God in the Bureau. Nor will I disobey orders and keep our ships and our people here if the government continues to negotiate in bad faith."

"We know that, Marc," Izaguirre said. "Believe me, I understand why you've taken this stance. The Bureau has had too much unchecked power for much too long and Watchman was the worst of them. I doubt there's a member sitting on it who isn't either in his pocket or one of his victims. They'd rather turn their backs on the system than risk having their secrets come out."

"Your thoughts, Colonel?" Nelms asked as the transport pulled through the embassy gates.

"Essential diplomatic personnel are to move to the safe rooms, sir. All others are to continue being evacced. I want you on a shuttle that is primed for lift off." She shook her head when he started to interrupt. "Secretary Nelms, my orders are clear and they come from Admiral Tremayne, General Okafor and the President. I am to keep you safe. That means you will transport back to the fleet if Vreman is one second late in responding to your deadline."

He didn't like it but she was right. Just not for the reasons she thought. He had to prove to the Midlothians that he wasn't running a bluff with them.

"How about a compromise, Colonel?" He smiled slightly when she narrowed her eyes in suspicion. "No shuttle but we will go to the safe room. However, we will move to the shuttle ten minutes before time runs out for Vreman. Will that work?"

She didn't like it and made no attempt to hide it. But, instead of arguing, she nodded once. "Your word that both of you will go to the shuttle the moment I tell you to without argument or delay." She pinned both he and Izaguirre with a firm look.

"You have our word," Nelms said and Izaguirre nodded in agreement.

He hoped it didn't come to that. He didn't want the deaths of Midlothian innocents weighing on him the rest of his life.

---

VREMAN THREW his glass across the room. The sound of it shattering against the far wall cut through the sounds of raised voices. Heads turned in his direct as silence fell. At the same time, he cursed loudly enough for everyone to hear. He didn't care if they knew he was furious. They'd wasted invaluable time arguing amongst themselves after Nelms left. Each minute wasted was one minute closer to their doom.

"Shut the fuck up." He ground out the words as he took a mental roll call. He fought the urge to curse again as he realized Reyes was no longer present. Sometime after Nelms left, the man had slipped out.

*Probably running in hopes of saving his sorry skin.*

"Sit down."

"We can't give in to them," Omar Ubacke said from his place down the table.

Vreman looked at the Finance Minister and frowned. He'd known the man was in Watchman's hip pocket. He had to be. There was no other way the former Intelligence Czar could have paid for all his "little projects". The fact they were all, to one degree or another, in Watchman's pocket didn't matter. Not now. Not when they needed to find a way to save themselves and the system.

"I assume you have a way out of the system then, Ubacke." He sneered at the man as Ubacke paled and shook his head. "It is fair to say we all would prefer it if Alexander Watchman was never found and never heard from again."

Heads nodded.

"However, ask yourselves this: are you willing to sacrifice everything—your lives, the lives of your loved ones and the lives of everyone in the system—to keep your secrets from coming out?"

No one spoke. More than a few of those gathered looked down, guilt radiating off them. He understood. But this went beyond the ten of them in the room. They'd made their play for power and it had been a good game while it lasted. All they could do now was comply with the Fuerconese demands and pray they somehow managed to claw their way out of the morass when the war was over.

Besides, if he played this right, he'd be able to pass the blame on betraying Watchman off on the other members of the Bureau and keep the man off his back. That would be a win-win situation.

"We still control the media. Even if Fuercon and her allies reveal anything they learn from Watchman or his files, we can deny it. It will be the word of a traitor against us. The public will believe us but only if we do everything possible to keep them safe from the Callusians."

One by one, heads nodded.

"Are we agreed then? We send word to Nelms that we will do what he asks and we follow through with that agreement."

He waited until everyone agreed. "Bethany, send the message and pray we aren't too late."

She stood and moved across the room to do as he said.

"Now, does anyone know where Reyes disappeared to?"

More head shakes and a few furtive looks. Well, he'd deal with them later, after this crisis. For now, he punched a code into his comm. A moment later, the door opened and Major Rudolph stepped inside.

"Major, send teams out to locate and arrest Santos Reyes on charges of treason and aiding and abetting the enemy. He is to be brought here as soon as you have him in custody."

"Yes, sir!"

"And inform your people that they are to share all information they have gathered in their investigation into the activities of Alexander Watchmen with the Fuerconese. That includes allowing them full access to all of Watchman's former holdings and files."

"Understood, Chairman."

"And find Watchman and kill that bastard before our *allies*." He spat out the word. "Get their hands on him."

"Sir?"

"You heard me, Major. Dismissed." He waited until Waas finished her call. Then he arched one brow in question. "Secretary Nelms and party will be here within the hour."

"Good. I suggest we use the time to prepare a sufficiently apologetic statement for him. We are begging not only for our lives but for the lives of everyone in this system."

"What if he's bluffing?" Yun Chin, head of their judiciary, asked.

"Marc Nelms doesn't bluff," Waas said. "Check the drone feeds from near the Fuerconese embassy. Their shuttles are on standby, those that haven't already left the planet. They have evacuated most of their staff and dependents. So have their allies. Trust me, their message is very clear. Either we play by their rules or we are on our own against the Callusians."

Vreman returned to his chair and sat. There was a great deal to do and not much time to do it before Nelms returned. God, life would be so much easier if Major Rudolph would find and deal—permanently and lethally—with Watchman before anything else happened.

# STAND AND FIGHT

## 15

*ATLANTIS RISING,* FLAGSHIP
  *First Fleet, Fuerconese Navy*
  *Midlothian space*


MIRANDA TREMAYNE PUSHED the plate to one side and reached for her datapad. Part of her wished the fleet had left the system days ago. She shook her head, a frown pulling at the corners of her mouth. The truth was she wished they'd never come to the system. Even so, she understood why they had and why they were still there. One part of her even agreed with the decision. The last thing she wanted was the destruction of a system on her conscience. But she hated the waiting and the wondering of when—not if—the Callusians would strike.

The last week had been non-stop. Nelms shuttled down to the surface each morning to meet with the Midlothian Administrative Bureau. Major Khan and his people assured her the Midlothians had finally opened their intelligence files on Watchman, holding little, if anything, back. The intelligence officer felt sure they were closing in on the former Intelligence Czar but they both knew they were fighting against time. If they didn't find the man before the Callusians hit the system, they'd lose him in the confusion that followed.

Worse, the reports coming in from FleetCom showed an increase in Callusian activity. If there was any good news, it was that there had been no further reports the enemy had deployed the biotoxin. Not that it reassure her. She operated under the assumption the Callusians planned on making an example of Midlothian. That meant using the biotoxin against the system. Worse, that meant her people could, and possibly would, fall victim as well.

She reached for her comm and entered a quick code.

"Yes, Admiral?" Captain Kohler said a moment later.

"New orders. All ships are to go to Protocol Alpha. I repeat Protocol Alpha." Sensors hadn't reported the enemy presence yet, but her gut told her their time was up. "Activate the sensor arrays and bring the defense platforms online."

"Admiral?"

"No, Raoul, I haven't received information you don't have. I'm playing a hunch. Better to be safe than sorry."

"Yes, ma'am. Protocol Alpha is active. I repeat, Protocol Alpha is active. Comms, pass the order on to all ships."

Tremayne listened as the comms officer did as instructed.

"Next order," Captain Kohler said. "Weapons, Sensors, bring defense and sensor arrays online. Inform Captain Middleton he has secondary command."

The orders were repeated.

"Captain, send for the secondary bridge crew. Once all posts are covered, primary crew is dismissed to get into light armor. All on-duty and essential personnel are to be armored according to their assignments until further orders." She stood and moved to her locker. "I'll report to the flag bridge as soon as I've followed my own orders."

"Yes, ma'am."

She ended the comm and began stripping out of her uniform. She tapped her earbud and requested a link to Ashlyn.

"Shaw."

"Ash, what's your situation?" She winced slightly as she finished the more unpleasant part of armoring up.

"Status quo, Admiral." The colonel spoke softly to someone and Tremayne listened as she moved away from whomever it had been. "Sorry, Admiral. Is there something I need to be aware of?"

"Nothing on sensors but my gut is telling me things are about to get interesting."

"Orders?"

"We've gone to Protocol Alpha and I've ordered defense and sensor arrays to go live."

Ash fell silent. "Miranda, I'm going to extract Nelms and Izaguirre from their meeting and throw them onboard a shuttle if necessary to get them back to the flagship."

"Good." She opened her mouth to say something only to be cut off as red alert sounded. "Damn it!"

"Admiral?" Concern filled Ashlyn's voice.

"One moment." She muted the channel and activate her link to the battlenet. "Update."

"Outer sensors picking up engine signatures indicating a Callusian taskforce or fleet translating into the system," Kohler said.

"Notify the ships in-system. Shields up and weapons ready. Notify our other assets to stand ready but not to break cover until my order."

"Aye aye, Admiral."

"Ash, we've picked up readings that seem to indicate the Callusians are translating in-system."

"I'll make sure the Marines are ready, ma'am."

"Colonel, get Nelms and Izaguirre to safety now!" she ordered as the battlenet came to life with a new wave of reports.

"Do we have time to get them to the shuttle and back to the ship?"

Tremayne didn't answer right away. She listened to the reports and did some mental math. Protocol demanded their people stay dirt-side. The danger of being caught in the middle of a firefight in a shuttle was too great. But she wanted Nelms onboard the flagship before the enemy attacked. The problem was she didn't know how long they had. So she couldn't risk Nelms making the trip—yet. But, if

CIC felt there was time for Nelms to return to the ship, she would order it. She would also order Ashlyn to join him. She needed the younger woman onboard to coordinate the Marine arm of the attack.

"Information is just now starting to come in, Ash. Get Nelms and his party back to the embassy. Once you have, I should have a better idea of what we're facing."

"Understood. Admiral." She paused and Tremayne pictured her making sure no one could overhear. "Miranda, don't do anything foolish."

"You take your own advice. Now get moving. Let me know as soon as you're back to the embassy."

"Aye, ma'am. Shaw out."

Tremayne turned her attention back to armoring up. As she did, she listened to the various reports coming in over the battlenet. Hopefully, the additional sensor arrays had sounded the alert early enough to give them time to prepare for anything the enemy had planned.

She grabbed her sidearm and slid it into place at her right thigh. Then, with one last check of her armor, she left her office. This is what they'd prepared for and what she'd prayed wouldn't happen. Now she needed to trust her people to do their duties and pray she had the wisdom and the cunning necessary to lead them to victory.

---

ASH ACTIVATED her link to the battlenet and listened to the reports coming in. For not the first time, she knew how lucky they were to have Tremayne in command of the mission. The admiral understood the enemy in a way very few in the Navy or FleetCom did. She also knew the importance of learning from her fellow officers. That was why she hadn't hesitated to adopt and adapt the tactics Admiral Collins used in the Savitar VI System. She may have saved the fleet by doing so.

Doing her best not to draw attention to herself, Ash moved to where Anisimova stood next to the door. The sergeant major had accompanied her that morning when she escorted the Secretary of

State dirtside. Now, as she approached, Anisimova's eyes narrowed and concern flickered over her expression. It was so quick no one would have caught it unless they'd been looking for it.

"We're moving out now. Tie into the battlenet." Ash spoke softly. "Once out of the conference room, you have the ambassador. Get him to the embassy no matter what. Understood?"

The blonde nodded once. As she did, her hand dropped to the sidearm secured to her left thigh.

Satisfied, Ash turned back to the room. Nelms sat at the far end of the table, Izaguirre next to him. They listened as Major Rudolph described the latest attempts to locate Watchman. She had to admit the intelligence officer was good, at least when it came to trying to sway the politicians. But she knew his tricks. Rico Santiago taught her to recognize them long ago.

"Mr. Secretary." She bent and spoke softly into Nelms' ear. "Forward sensor arrays have picked up what Admiral Tremayne feels certain are the leading edges of a Callusian element. It's time to go, sir."

He nodded, his expression never changing. Then he stood. Surprised, Izaguirre quickly followed suit. At Ashlyn's signal, Anisimova stepped forward, taking her place next to the ambassador. Time was ticking and Ash knew they needed to move.

"Ladies and gentlemen, Admiral Tremayne just sent word that her sensors have picked up what appears to be the leading edges of a Callusian incursion into the system," Nelms said.

Someone down the table gasped. Several others cursed. But each of them paled as the seriousness of the situation struck them.

"The admiral has brought the taskforce to alert status. I recommend you sound the alert and get your citizens to shelter."

"Mr. Secretary, we need to leave."

Ash took his arm and, not leaving him any choice, escorted him out of the room. The moment they entered the outer office, the rest of the escort team fell into place, surrounding the two diplomats. The Marines had secured their battle helmets in place. Ash lifted her left arm, the fingers of her right hand entering the command sequence on her armor's control pad to activate her helmet. It slid up and over her head and she inhaled quickly as the faceplate slid into place. It was always a bit disorientating when the helmet sealed itself into place. Then the armor's systems came online and her HUD began streaming data.

"What's going on?" Izaguirre asked as the Marines checked every corner before letting them to progress.

"It looks like the Callusians are making their play." Nelms looked at Ashlyn in surprise when she ordered them to bypass the elevators, taking the stairs instead.

"Too dangerous if the enemy manages to break through our defenses, sir," Anisimova said before Ash could explain. "Titan, Friar, take point. Ranger, Rider, you've got our six."

The four Marines peeled off and assumed their positions.

"Let's go." Ash once again reached for Nelms' arm, keeping him close to her side as they entered the stairwell. Until they were safely back to the embassy, she planned on keeping him within arm's reach.

"Transport's waiting just outside the gates, Colonel," Anisimova said as they emerged onto the ground floor.

"Let's move. Gentlemen, run!"

The sight of the Marine detail escorting the two diplomats through the lobby and outside at a dead run brought everyone else to a stop. She spared them a moment's thought. Then she guided Nelms outside. Four Marines waited for them next to a heavily armored transport. Ash shoved the Secretary of State inside and stepped away so Izaguirre could follow. Then she dove in after them, waiting as the rest of the Marines followed suit.

"Reacher, get us back to the embassy and step on it," Anismova ordered.

"Colonel?"

"Sir, Admiral Tremayne has brought the fleet to alert. Weapons and shields are live as are the sensor and defense arrays. My orders are to get the two of you safely back to the embassy. By then, the admiral will have a better handle on the situation. If she feels we can do so safely, you will then be removed to the flagship. Otherwise, you will be secured in the main saferoom until this is over."

"Our people?" Izaguirre asked.

"Most everyone has already been transported shipboard. Unless I'm very much mistaken, the admiral has their ships in the middle of the formation in order to protect them during the attack."

"Colonel, we're nearing the embassy," the driver said.

"Straight back to the shuttles. Everyone is to hold position until Admiral Tremayne confirms our orders." She opened a comm to the flagship.

"Status?" Tremayne asked.

"We just cleared the embassy gates."

"Any trouble?"

"Not so far. Secretary Nelms informed the Bureau members of the change in status and recommended they alert the public. So far, it doesn't appear they've done so."

"Correction, Colonel. The alert is going out now," Anisimova said.

Ash nodded and passed on the information.

"Things will start getting bad down there in fairly short order, Colonel. Button up the embassy and don't take any chances."

"Understood, Admiral." Ash glanced out of the transport as it braked to a stop near the waiting shuttles. "Do we bunker down or transport up?"

"Bunker down. We're still trying to get a handle on the situation here. Make sure the ambassador and Secretary Nelms are safe."

"Aye, Admiral."

"Update in half an hour, Colonel. Tremayne out."

Ashlyn turned to the driver. "Get us as close to the embassy as you can. Mr. Secretary, Ambassador, when I give the order, you are to move inside the building as quickly as you can. Don't detour anywhere. Head straight down to the safe room. My people will make sure the remaining staff are "

And heaven help them all if the Callusians use the biotoxin against the planet. They hadn't had time to test the safeguards they'd put into place.

"Durga," she said as two of the Marines led Nelms and Izaguirre out of the transport. "We need to prepare for attempts to breach the perimeter. If the public realizes we have shuttles still groundside, there might be attempts to hijack them."

"Should we move the birds inside the hangar?"

"See what the pilots think. If they feel they can hold the shuttles in readiness there and not delay our departure by doing so, then yes. Otherwise, use whatever means necessary to keep those birds safe. I need to make sure Nelms and Izaguirre are safely stowed."

Ten minutes later, Ash stood in the main safe room deep below the embassy. Fortunately for the fifteen men and women ranged around the room, Ambassador Izaguirre had taken the first warnings about the biotoxin to heart. He'd done all he could to implement the new protocols. Backup environmental systems that did not connect to the outside, or even to the upper floors of the embassy, would be turned on when she left the room, securing the door behind her. They had enough power, food and water to last a month. More if they were careful. That would be long enough for help to come if the worst happened.

"Mr. Secretary, you will have an open comm link to me and to the flagship. Once I leave these rooms, you are all going to be sealed in. Do not try to break the seal until we give you the all-clear."

"Colonel, you and your people need to bunker down," Nelms said.

"Sir, our duty is to keep you, the ambassador and every man and woman in here with you safe. Our armor will protect us." She hoped. So far, the best they had was seeing how the upgrades worked on Shennong. The biotoxin had several weeks to dissipate by then. She hoped they did as well with the chemical at full strength, assuming the Callusians managed to disperse on the capital.

"You're sure there's not time to get us to the ships?" one of the ambassador's aides asked from the back of the main room.

"Admiral Tremayne feels we are all safer down here, sir." Didn't he understand she would much prefer being in space or with a boarding party? "However, she will re-evaluate the situation when she knows more. If there is a change in status, we'll let Secretary Nelms know."

"We will do as you say, Colonel," Nelms assured her.

"Thank you, sir." She listened as Anisimova reported on the status topside. "Corporal Stannis will remain here with you. If you have any questions or any concerns, let him know. For now, settle in. If we're lucky, this is a feint by the enemy, and we'll have all of you up to the fleet soon."

She shook hands with first Nelms and then Izaguirre. Then she had a last word with Stannis, reminding him not to let the civilians run roughshod over him.

"Durga, I'm on my way topside." She watched the reinforced door slide into place and entered the lockdown sequence on the keypad in the wall. "Status?"

"The shuttles have been moved into the bay. Lt. Keneshaw assures me they can keep the engines on standby and it won't delay our departure. Drones are up and all defenses are active. Spider is monitoring civilian comms. The government has finally issued a bunker in place order. Begging the colonel's pardon but, for the most part, it looks like the warning is ignored."

Ash frowned and shook her head. That was the problem with civilians. They either panicked or they ignored the warning. Both reactions got people killed. While it wasn't her concern just then, she mourned what she feared would happen when the attack finally came.

"All right. New orders. If the embassy grounds are breached, all Marines are to regroup on the secure level. We will lock down the lifts and hold our ground there. Make sure everyone understands."

"Roger that."

"And, from this point forward, we go to call signs. Full battlefield protocol. Weapons hot."

"Call signs, full battlefield protocol and weapons hot, aye."

Satisfied, Ash stepped onto the lift and programmed it for the ground floor. As she did, she went over her mental checklist for situations like this one. They'd done all they could, at least until they knew more.

"Angel." Anisimova fell into step next to her as she stepped off the lift. "Command center has been set up in the ambassador's office and Admiral Tremayne asked you to comm her with your report."

"Any word from Vreman or anyone else from the Bureau?"

A bitter smile twisted the sergeant major's lips. "Several members have commed, demanding we take them in and transport them to one of our ships."

"And your response?"

"I respectfully declined, pointing out that we were currently grounded just like they were."

"I take it they didn't like your reply."

"You could say that." Her eyes flashed. "Angel, they will sell us out if they think it buys them another day."

"I know." She turned into Izaguirre's office and shook her head. In the short time since their return to the embassy, the office had been transformed. It was now a workable command center. Too bad it didn't have a fully stocked armory as well. "Let me report to Tremayne. Hopefully, she'll have some good news."

"Colonel, is your position secure?" Tremayne's image appeared on the small screen on the desk a short time later.

"For the moment, Admiral. Secretary Nelms, Ambassador Izaguirre and the remaining staff are locked in the safe room below the embassy. Corporal Stannis is with them. I've locked down the rest of the embassy and activated its defenses. The shuttles are on standby."

"And the situation with the local populace?"

"The Bureau issued a shelter in place advisory. For the most part, it is being ignored. My people have been checking with allied embassies and those who still have personnel dirtside have also gone to lock-down status."

"What's your assessment of the situation?"

"Right now, we're safe. But you know what will happen if this proves to be more than a feint by the enemy. All hell's going to break loose down here as panic sets in."

The admiral nodded grimly. "CIC doesn't feel this is a feint, Colonel. The approach vector is such that the enemy ships will be in position to fire on the capital within three hours if they maintain their current speed. They will enter our weapons envelop in two hours."

Ash mentally cursed. There was time, barely, to get everyone to the ships but doing so would leave the fleet open to attack because they would have to lower their shields for the shuttles to dock. It was a no-win situation.

"I understand, ma'am." And she did.

"Understand this as well, Colonel. We've received demands from the Midlothian government for us to evacuate members of the Administrative Bureau. Chairman Vreman said failure to do so means we are in breach of our agreements with his government."

"I see." And she did. "He, as well as other members of the Bureau, have made the same demands of Sergeant Major Anisimova. She informed them we are as beached as they are. They were not amused."

"Do you think they will try to force the issue?"

"I do, Admiral. I also feel they won't hesitate to sell the fleet out if they believe it will save their skins."

"Very well. You are to hold your post, Colonel. Your first duty is to keep our diplomats safe. However, if anyone attempts to take action against the embassy, you are authorized to use whatever means you feel necessary to turn back the attack. Am I clear?"

Ash knew better than to ask any questions. Tremayne had given her the opening she needed to do whatever it took to protect the embassy and prevent the members of the Bureau from betraying them. If, in the process, she managed to cut off the head of the snake leading the conspiracy against Fuercon and her allies, all the better.

"Very clear, Admiral." She looked up as Anisimova appeared in the doorway. "One moment, Admiral. The sergeant major just joined me."

"Begging your pardon, Admiral, Colonel, but we've received another demand from Vreman."

"Colonel, I leave it to you to deal with him. Tag me if you need me to back you on anything. Tremayne out."

Ash smiled grimly. Tremayne's message was clear. She would deal with the battle in space. Ash and her Marines were to deal with the headache of the members of the Bureau. Before she decided how to do so, she needed to hear what Vreman had to say.

"Put him through, Durga."

She sat back and waited. A moment later, Vreman's image appeared on her screen. Gone was the assured man she'd seen the last several days during his negotiations with Nelms. Fear and desperation replaced self-assurance.

"Colonel Shaw, where is Secretary Nelms?" Vreman's expression betrayed how much he did not want to talk to her.

"The Secretary, as well as the remainder of the embassy staff, are secure in a safe room, Chairman, where they will remain until the danger is over." She let him consider that for a moment. "How may I help you, Chairman?"

"What are you going to do to protect us, Colonel?"

She arched one brow. Then she sat up, letting him see she wasn't intimidated by him. "Sir, we are doing exactly as Secretary Nelms told you we would. The elements of First Fleet in-system will do everything possible to prevent the Callusians from successfully attacking. In the meantime, my Marines will do all they can to protect Secretary Nelms, Ambassador Izaguirre and the remaining members of the embassy staff still on-planet."

"That's not enough!" Panic shone in his eyes. "You must evacuate the Administrative Bureau to one of your ships."

"Really?" She didn't try to hide her contempt. "Mr. Vreman, consider the danger doing so would put the Bureau members in if the enemy were to launch an attack before the shuttle could dock with one of the ships. Consider the optics of the move as well. How will your constituents look on it if they learned you and your cohorts chose to leave the planet, abandoning them in the process. Finally, ask yourself this: why would I give any consideration to tying up one of our shuttles and pilots to evacuate you and the others when Secretary Nelms, not to mention the rest of the embassy staff as well as my own people, is stuck here?" She chopped a hand in front of her, cutting off his next comment.

"Mr. Vreman, hear me. Our ships will do everything possible to protect the system. However, if you consider for even a moment selling us out to the enemy, Admiral Tremayne won't hesitate to withdraw our forces from the system and leave you to the Callusians' tender mercies. Are you willing to run that risk?"

"She'd be leaving you as well," he sneered.

"Sir, that is a sacrifice every Marine under my command is aware of and willing to make. We will die if necessary to protect this embassy and those under our protection. Can you say the same?"

She waited, watching as he processed what she said.

"While you consider that, Mr. Vreman, consider this as well. The current events do not change the fact Fuercon still expects you to turn over Alexander Watchman. Since I assume you are sheltering in place, there is no reason your people can't continue feeding what information you have to our intel officers."

"You bitch!"

"Negative, sir. I assure you my parents were married when I was born." She smiled as he gaped at her. "What I am is a member of the Fuerconese Marine Corps determined to carry out my duties." She ended the transmission and chuckled softly. "I wonder how long it will be before he tries to reach Nelms directly?"

"My guess?" Anisimova's eyes sparkled with amusement. "After he changes his pants. He didn't expect you to call his bluff."

Ash grinned. Then she stood. Even though they were in a wait and see situation, there was still a great deal to be done. That began by having a word with Major Khan.

"Sitrep?" she asked Anisimova.

"The drones are up and we're getting constant feeds from them. The automated security measures have been activated. I've ordered our people to take up posts at the main entrance and at the entrance leading to the hangar. Two Marines are guarding the shuttles and the shuttle pilots are bunking hot there. Major Khan and his people are setting up camp in the waiting room outside the safe room."

Ashlyn nodded in approval. "I'm going to do a walkthrough to check things myself. Get with Khan and let him know he has full authorization to not only monitor the public broadcasts but hack into the government comms. Officially, he's looking for anything linking back to Watchman. Unofficially, he and his people are to be looking for anything that indicates the Midlothians are going to turn against us. I'll take any heat for it if it comes back on us."

"The politicians here might scream a bit but none of our people will give you any grief over it," the blonde said.

Ash merely shrugged. She knew firsthand how quickly the political tide could turn. When it did, politicians looked for scapegoats. She had no intention of letting any of her people fill that role. If that meant standing between them and those screaming for blood, she would. This time, however, she wouldn't sit quietly as the politicians tried to railroad her. Hopefully, it wouldn't come to that.

"Tell Howler to maintain a constant check on the battlenet. He's to tag me and then you of any status change."

"Roger that."

"We'll meet back here in fifteen." Hopefully, that would be long enough for her to do her own check of their security.

"Watch your six, Angel."

"You too, Durga."

They'd all better watch their sixes until this was over.

# 16

*ATLANTIS RISING, FLAGSHIP*
  *First Fleet, Fuerconese Navy*
  *Midlothian space*

"ADMIRAL, CIC REPORT INCOMING," the comms officer said.

Miranda Tremayne crossed the flag bridge to stand behind the young man. "Put it through."

"Ruzek here, Admiral. We have new readings on the incoming ships. I can report with confidence these are Callusian ships. Sensors identified at least five as having taken part in the attack on the Bennington System."

"Number of bogies?"

"Still refining that information but our current count stands at more than twenty. Four battlecruisers, half a dozen destroyers, five frigates and a mix of smaller craft. While we're fairly confident in those numbers, it is possible there are other ships shadowing those that we have yet to identify."

Even though she wanted to frown, she didn't. The numbers were larger than she'd have liked, especially since she had to consider at least one or more of the ships carried missiles loaded with the biotoxin. But it could be worse, much worse. "Have you been able to strip their IDs yet?"

"Negative, Admiral. The IDs we have are based on engine read-outs, so they aren't guaranteed."

"All right, Commander. Pass the information on to the rest of our ships." She ended the comm and returned to her command chair. For a long moment, she studied the holo plot. This was always the part of battle preparation she hated. Decisions made now would impact the start of the fight and, if she made the wrong choices, could lead to a quick defeat. "New orders. LACs and battle shuttles for our leading elements are to go hot and standby for the launch order. Unless there is a change in status, all ships are to bring up shields in fifteen minutes. The *Corrigan* is to hail the incoming ships at that time. If there is no response, a warning shot is to follow. Tight beam message to the rest of the fleet. They are to standby for my order to move in. Operation Pincer will commence at that time."

She listened as the orders were repeated back before being sent back. Then she glanced at the time. If nothing changed, the enemy would be in weapons range in an hour. She could try closing the distance and forcing the issue or she could hold position. There were pros and cons to both approaches. There was one factor, however, that overrode everything else—the need to protect the system. Her ships and their assets were in the best possible positions to meet the attack. Assuming, of course, the Callusians didn't have additional ships waiting to enter the battle.

"Get me Colonel Shaw."

Hopefully, she would have some good news.

---

"Sir, change in enemy status."

Commander Diogo Fryxell leaned forward, studying the plot. His upper lip peeled back into an almost feral smile as his eyes narrowed. He'd warned High Command the danger of moving on the system so soon after the other attacks. Between that and the almost direct line the attacks had taken place on, they'd all but handed the Midlothians notice of their intent to invade. Now it was up to him to bring the system to heel. The only point of negotiation was the system's immediate surrender. Once he had that in hand, he would conscript its military and manufacturing centers. High Command had been clear. The system was to be punished but not destroyed. Unfortunately, it looked like that might not be a possibility.

"Do we have an ID on the ships?" His tone informed everyone in earshot that they'd better have one. Otherwise, heads would roll, quite possibly literally.

"Preliminary identification suggests they are elements of the Fuerconese First Fleet."

Fryxell fisted one hand in frustration. Fuercon's First and Second Fleets had been the bane of Callusian existence for years. Between the two, they had dealt the Callusian Navy more defeats the rest of the allied navies combined. It was just his luck to run into one of them here. Well, they didn't know what he had in store for them.

An evil smile touched his lips and he pushed out of his chair. "Inform the Weapons Master to prepare the special loads. Let's give them a taste of what we can do."

Not only should that convince the damned Fuerconese to stay out of their business, but it would act as a warning for the Midlothians. They either went along with his demands or he'd turn the biotoxin loose on their capital planet.

"Bring all ships to alert. Time to firing range?"

"Sixty-two minutes, sir."

"Time until we enter their weapons' envelope?"

"Forty-six minutes."

He frowned. Somehow, he needed to take that advantage away from the enemy. Otherwise, his ships lost the element of surprise. Not that they really had it to begin with. Still, if the Fuerconese had one weakness, it was their belief in fair play. The enemy commander wouldn't open fire until they'd gone through the motions of making sure his ships presented a threat. By then, it would be too late. He would see to it.

"Inform the flight captain that he is to launch the first set of LACs at the forty minute mark. They are to launch counter-measures to blind the enemy sensors at the forty-five minute mark."

The comms officer once again repeated the orders before passing them on. As he did, Fryxell leaned back and considered his options. There was one hold card he hadn't brought into play yet. Perhaps it was time to do so.

"I'll be in my ready room." With that, he stood and left the bridge, trusting the crew to contact him if there was any change in status. It was time to make sure certain members of the Midlothian government understood exactly what their options were.

---

"Colonel, you might want to listen to this."

Ashlyn moved to stand at Major Khan's shoulder. As she did, the intelligence specialist nodded to the woman sitting next to him. She input a code and a moment later, a voice with an unmistakable accent filled the room.

"Do you know who this is, Mr. Watchman?"

"I know what you are," a second voice responded.

Ashlyn's eyes went wide. Then she looked at Khan. The major nodded once, confirming it was the former Intelligence Czar.

"I want his location," she ordered softly as she waited for the message to continue.

"You know the current situation, Mr. Watchman." The Callusian didn't wait for confirmation before continuing. "If you want your planet to survive, you will convince your government to turn against the Fuerconese presence and use system defenses to clear our path."

"If you know the current situation—and I assume you do—then you know that isn't possible. The way certain members of your navy mishandled things with Fuercon and her allies revealed our alliance.

Not only have I been stripped of my office but I have a price on my head."

"That is your problem. You have thirty-five minutes to convince them to do as I said or we will lay waste to the entire system. How will you feel as you watch the biotoxin destroying your homeworld? There will be nowhere safe. You can hide but it will find you and you will be just as dead as everyone else."

"There's another minute or so of the exchange before it ends," Khan said. "Basically, more threats from the Callusian and more excuses from Watchman."

"Do you have an ID?"

"We're running that now."

"Copy it to the flag." She considered for a moment. "Did you get a location on Watchman?"

"Still working on it, Colonel," Lt. Okumura said. She paused, her head cocked to one side. "Watchman's making a call."

Ashlyn's brows winged up. Before she could say anything, Khan instructed the lieutenant to let them hear it.

"You know better than to contact me here," a woman's voice hissed in anger.

"Listen and we might both live to see morning," Watchman said. "Our *friends*." He spat out the word. "Contacted me. They weren't please to find we have guests and suggested action be taken to clear them out. Things are a bit crowded here."

*Get me his location*, Ash mouthed to Khan.

"How do you expect me to do that?" the unseen woman asked.

"There are certain platforms you can use to support the argument that they've outstayed their welcome."

He was good. Ashlyn had to give him that. Most people hearing the conversation wouldn't guess he'd just told the woman to use the system's defense platforms against their ships. What he didn't know, what the woman hopefully didn't know, was that they'd anticipated that move and had taken steps to prevent it from happening. But Tremayne needed to be updated. She might have an idea on how best to proceed.

Ash frowned as she listened to another quick exchange between Watchman and the woman. As she did, she leaned forward. She could almost recognize the woman's voice.

Who was she?

"Are you crazy? If I do what you want, there will be nothing standing between us and the Callusians."

"If you don't, the Callusians will destroy everything," Watchman countered.

"I'll get back to you." Silence fell and Ash waited, wondering if either of them would say anything else. "And don't contact me here again."

The call ended. Ashlyn looked from Okumura to Khan. Both were busy inputting commands into their datapads. Knowing they were trying to get her an ID on the woman as well as Watchman's location, she left them to it and stepped out of the room. Khan would send for her once he had the information she wanted. In the meantime, she needed to let Tremayne know the latest developments.

"Talk to me, Ash," the admiral said a few moments later.

"Are we on a secure channel, ma'am?"

"We are."

Ash blew out a breath. "There have been a couple of developments you need to be aware of. Major Khan will be uploading some audio files to the flagship shortly. The first is a discussion between Watchman and a Callusian. I assume it is the Callusian commander. Watchman was instructed to find a way to force the government to use the defense platforms against our ships. Failure to do so would see them releasing the biotoxin on the capital planet."

"Well, that answers one question. Watchman is in-system."

"Not only in-system but in the capital from the sounds of it, Miranda." She paced a few steps and then stopped. "The second call was from Watchman to a member of the government. My guess is someone on the Bureau but I couldn't quite place the voice. Hopefully, either Khan and his team or someone on the ship can get an ID ASAP."

"Do you have a location on Watchman?"

"Working on it." She held up a hand when Khan appeared in the doorway. "One moment, Admiral. We might have something else."

"We have an ID, Colonel," Khan said as he handed over his datapad.

She scanned the information displayed. When she asked, he confirmed they'd double-checked their results. She thanked him and reopened the channel to Tremayne.

"Admiral, we have an ID on the person Watchman contacted. Bethany Waas."

Tremayne cursed softly. "All right. Colonel, you know the timeline we're operating under. I leave it to you to decide your best course of action at this time. I assure you we will take steps to make sure the platforms are secure. However, short of keeping at least some of our guns focused on groundside defenses, we can do little where they are concerned."

"Leave that to me, ma'am. I'm sure Major Khan and his team can be of assistance there. I'll keep you updated."

"Be careful, Ash. Tremayne out."

Ash closed her eyes and tipped her head back. She let her mind clear, knowing she needed to keep centered. When she opened her eyes a few moments later, Khan waited.

"Major Khan, the admiral expects us to do whatever we can to control the situation down here. She is concerned about the groundside defenses. Is there anything you and your people can do along those lines?"

"I do believe we can, ma'am." His grin was almost as evil as hers as she thought about how best to deal with Waas.

"Then get on it. Let me know if you need anything. I'm going to take a squad with me and pay Waas a visit."

"Begging your pardon, Colonel, but what the fuck do you think you're going to do?" Anisimova's voice as she joined them was soft and deadly.

Ashlyn looked at her and flinched. She recognized the master sergeant's expression and knew it boded no good. At least not for her.

"Perhaps I should have said you and I were going to take a squad," she hedged.

Anisimova frowned a moment longer and then nodded.

"You have command here until we return, Major. We'll take one of the armored transports. Have one shuttle ready to respond to our location if necessary."

"Understood, ma'am."

"Button the embassy up tight once we leave. Do not open up for anyone until we return."

"Yes, ma'am."

"Raven, I wouldn't go if I didn't know you can handle this. I'll make sure Colonel Santiago knows how invaluable you and your team have been on the mission." She shook his hand. "Durga, put a squad together. Full battle rattle. We're going to pay a visit to Bethany Waas."

"Ma'am?"

"I'll brief you once we're on our way. But the short version is she was just in contact with Watchman and my money is on her knowing where he is. That, however, is secondary right now to the fact she may be about to betray our ships."

Anisimova's mouth pulled down into a frown and anger flashed in her eyes. Then she nodded and pulled her comm. A moment later, she gave Ash a nod. "The squad will meet us at the shuttle."

"Then let's go. The clock's ticking."

With that, Ashlyn headed down the corridor to their makeshift armory. Things were about to get interesting and she planned to be prepared for any possibility.

## 17

"YOU CAN'T GO INSIDE."

The man stood in front of Waas' office door. Even though his hand rested on his sidearm, Ash could all but hear his knees knocking. Not that she blamed him. Four armed and armored Fuerconese Marines, Devil Dogs every one, stood in front of them. Their weapons, unlike his, were in hand. He didn't stand a chance against them, but she'd prefer it not to come down to that.

"You can step aside or we will move you. It is imperative I have a moment of Secretary Waas' time," she said.

"I can't. You don't have authorization."

Ash shook her head, a slight smile on her lips. "That hasn't stopped us so far and it won't stop us now." She motioned the one member of the squad in heavy armor forward. "Hound, if you please."

"With pleasure, ma'am." He reached out and easily lifted the guard away from the door. "Stay." He placed a gloved hand in the middle of the man's chest, holding him in place.

"My turn, Angel," Boomer said.

The demolitions specialist stepped forward and gently nudged Ashlyn to the side. He quickly scanned the door and then shook his head, a look of disappointment on his face. Ashlyn chuckled softly as he stepped back and kicked open the door, knowing he would have much preferred using some of his beloved explosives.

Before Ash could enter, Anisimova stopped her. At the sergeant major's order, Hound and Boomer entered first, weapons at the ready. By the time Ashlyn stepped inside, the squad had four people, including Waas, secured. Ash moved forward, Anisimova at her side, studying the four.

"How dare you!" Waas struggled to break free from Boomer's grip.

"Quiet!" Ashlyn motioned for one of the squad to guard the door. She didn't want anyone interrupting their *discussion.* "I'm going to make this short and sweet because time is running out. Bethany Waas, approximately twenty minutes ago, you received a comm from Alexander Watchman. His comments to you left no doubt that he has been in contact with the Callusian invasionary force. He instructed you to turn your defense platforms against our ships. Your response revealed a great deal. First, you weren't surprised to hear from. You weren't happy, but you also weren't surprised. Nor were you surprised to hear from him. That leads me to assume you've been in contact with him not only after he was removed from office but after we arrived in-system. Finally, you did not tell him you refused to work with the Callusians. Instead, you said you would get back to him.

"If that's not bad enough, y failed to contact Admiral Tremayne or Secretary Nelms after the call. That leaves me no choice but to conclude two things. First, you have been an active conspirator against not only your home system but against Fuercon and her allies. Second, you meant to do as Watchman said. That makes you an enemy combatant. We're here to take you and anyone working with you against the best interests of Fuercon and this system into custody."

"No!" Waas kicked back, wincing as her heel collided with Boomer's armor. "You can't. We're just trying to save our system." A tear actually appeared in one of her eyes.

"I can and I will." At Ashlyn's nod, Boomer secured the woman's hands behind her back and forced her to her knees. "And I assume what you just said that these others are as involved in the betrayal as you are. Sergeant Major, please inform Admiral Tremayne and Secretary Nelms that we have taken Wass as well as Vreman, Reyes and Erdogan into custody. Secretary Nelms can inform whoever takes over as head of the Bureau of our actions and the reasons why."

"Secure the rest of them," the blonde ordered Boomer and Hound before doing as Ash said.

"Each of you, listen very carefully. You have one chance and one chance only to mitigate your crimes against Midlothian as well as Fuercon and her allies. Where is Alexander Watchman?"

"You can't make us say anything," Vreman all but spat.

"True. But I can make sure you don't harm anyone else who was foolish enough to trust you to look after their best interests." She made a show of considering her options. "Take them to the lobby and secure them there. Make sure they won't be able to leave or call for help. Then break out the windows. Let them feel the fresh air."

Her upper lip curled back as Reyes teared up. "I want to make sure each of you have a front row seat to the destruction of the capital. After all, you've played a role in what's about to happen. As for us, we'll take our leave once you're secured and return to the fleet. We should have just about enough time to evacuate the rest of our people from the embassy and return to our ships before the enemy is withing weapons range. We can be out of the system before they have a chance to open fire. I imagine they won't be happy to have their ambush foiled and will want to make someone pay."

"No, please. Don't leave us to them," Waas pleaded.

"Convince me it's worth the risk to stay and deal with you."

"We don't know where Watchman is, Colonel. You have to believe us," Vreman said.

"Sorry, not good enough." She turned and started to the door. As she did, she heard the others hauling their prisoners to their feet.

"No!" Reyes screamed.

Ash chuckled as Boomer cursed and muttered something about the coward pissing himself. There might be someone in FleetCom who wouldn't approve of her tactics, but she didn't care. Time was running out and she didn't plan on being above ground when the fighting began. Not unless she could get back to the fleet.

"You heard the colonel, Marines. Let's go make these folks a tad bit more uncomfortable." Anismova's derision was clear.

"Wait!"

Ash turned. Vreman stood next to Waas. His expression as he looked at the woman was resigned. Waas shook her head. He glared and nodded once.

"Tell her," he said.

"He'll have moved on by now. He never stays in one place after he contacts one of us," the woman hedged.

"Tell me or take your chances with the Callusians and with your own people when they find out how you betrayed them." Ash waited, wondering how the woman would respond.

"All right. But if I do, you have to get us out of here."

"Oh, I will." She just wouldn't tell them where she planned to take them. Not until she had the information she wanted and had confirmed it. "You have sixty seconds to tell me or we're out of here." Ash made a show of checking her chrono.

With fifteen seconds remaining, Waas finally gave her an address.

"See, that wasn't too hard, was it. Think about all the trouble you could have saved yourselves if you'd cooperated earlier." She started toward the door and then stopped. "You heard?" she asked the security guard who had been hovering just outside.

He swallowed hard once and then nodded.

"I have no doubt you have an area where they can be secured for a short while."

Another nod.

"Boomer, Hound, secure them and then report to the transport. We're running out of time and I'd prefer to be able to tell the admiral the mission was successful."

"Roger that, Angel," Hound said and motioned for the guard to lead the way.

"What now?" Anisimova asked as the prisoners were led out of the office.

"We go for Watchman." She paused as the transport driver commed. "We need to get a move on. Racer says things are starting to get dicey on the streets as people realize the Callusians are really are closing in."

Hopefully, their luck would hold and they'd get their hands on Watchman before all hell broke loose. She did not want to have to fight her way through a bunch of panicked civilians in order to return to the embassy.

---

ALEXANDER WATCHMAN STARED at the live feed from the security cams outside the building. In the last half hour, the streets had gone from almost deserted to clogged with people and vehicles as panic set in. The government's order to shelter in place forgotten, they foolishly believed they had time to flee the upcoming onslaught. Fools! There would be no escape for them or anyone else. Not unless Waas and her fellow members of the Bureau decided to pull their heads out of the asses and do something. All they had to do was turn the defense platforms against the Fueronese ships. If they did, the Callusians would leave them alone.

Well, for the most part.

He turned away from the screen and considered his options. Whether he wanted to admit it or not, the Callusians would make an example of Midlothian. They believed the Bureau—and him—had betrayed them. They might not use the biotoxin against the entire planet, much less the entire system, but someone would pay the price. All he could do was watch and wait and pray they didn't choose Caspian Bay as their target.

Damn it, he shouldn't have waited so long before leaving the system. He knew better. But he thought he had more time. All he'd needed was another week or two. He had Waas, Reyes and several others on the Bureau in hand. He finally managed to bring Vreman to heel. Why in the hell did the Callusians have to make their move so soon?

Everything he'd worked for, everything he'd done to protect Midlothian and bring her into her rightful place as a power player in the galaxy had been for naught. Hell, his actions might be the reason why.

No, he couldn't and wouldn't believe that. This was the government's fault for not looking beyond the next trade deal and taking steps that should have been taken years ago. This was the fault of the allies, and especially the Fuerconese, for not ceding to the demands of the Callusians. He'd had everything worked out. But they screwed it up, just like they did everything else.

And now?

Now he should be safe deep within the capitol complex. But no. He couldn't go there without risking arrest—or worse. He'd gotten soft in his old age. He'd left too many enemies alive. Enemies who would gladly sign his death warrant. Now, with the Callusians beating on the proverbial door and Fuercon the only thing standing between them, those same enemies would bow to whatever Fuercon wanted if it meant living another day. He might as well put a pulsar to his head and pull the trigger.

But did he dare risk not using what pull he still had to make sure he—and his government—were safe.

Everything he'd done had been for Midlothian. If it meant his death to try one last time, so be it. But he'd take his own precautions first. He might be desperate but that didn't make him a fool. If anyone in the government tried anything, everything he'd gathered over the years, all the dirty little—and big—secrets would go public, after first finding their way to Fuercon and to all of Midlothian's so-called allies. Then the media and the public. He would see to it each and every one of them paid the price if they betrayed him.

---

"What's your status, Angel?"

Ash checked the external monitors before answering. "We're about to breach the last known location for Watchman. From there, we'll head back to the embassy."

"And the prisoners?"

"Secured in a cell at in the government house, ma'am. We, uh, reprogrammed the security system for it. They won't be let out any time soon unless it is by one of us."

"You have fifteen minutes to find your target and return to the embassy. After that, the enemy will be within weapons range."

"Understood." She switched to a private channel and secured her helmet. "Miranda, what's the status up there. The truth."

"We've issued the challenge. No response, not that I expected one. Weapons are at ready and the first volley will be away in ten minutes barring a change in status. You?"

"Things are getting dicey down here, as expected. But we should be able to do this in the time allotted."

She hoped.

"How confident are you of your information?"

"Not as confident as I'd like, Miranda, but it is the best lead yet." Mainly because it was their only lead. "Let's say I got a bit inventive with the prisoners in order to get them to talk."

"Ashlyn." Tremayne drawled out her name and Ash winced slightly. Just then, the admiral sounded like her mother whenever Elizabeth didn't approve of something she'd done.

"I promise we didn't lay a hand on any of them, Miranda, other than to secure them. No one was injured. But I did put the fear of God into them. It might have been mentioned that they possibly could have been left in an open air location where they'd have a front row seat to what happened if the biotoxin was released in the atmosphere."

Tremayne didn't quite hide her chuckle. "I'd say that wasn't stepping over the line and will make sure my report says so."

Ash closed her eyes and swallowed against the emotion that suddenly tightened her throat. Despite everything going on, Tremayne was doing what she could to protect Ash and her Marines.

"Thank you, ma'am."

"Get a move on, Ash. Time's running short."

"You watch your six, Miranda. They are here to make a point and you and the rest of the First would be a great big notch in their belt."

"You do the same." She paused and Ash listened in as a new series of reports came in over the battlenet. "Ash, if we can clear a window for you to get back safely to the fleet, we'll do it. Otherwise, get your ass back to the embassy and bunker down under full safety protocol. Getting Watchman or reclaiming the prisoners is not an imperative right now."

"Roger that. Shaw out." She took one last look at the building and then turned to Boomer. "Knock on the door, Boomer. Get us inside without any delay."

"Yes, ma'am."

The demolitions specialist shot her a grin before jumping out of the transport, Hound on his heels. The two armored Marines cut a path through the crowd jamming the street and sidewalk. The sight of Hound in full heavy armor, a rail gun in hand, sent the crowd pushing to the opposite side of the street. Ash shook her head, wishing they could do something to help those people. Unfortunately, because of the lack of action by the Midlothian government and the refusal to admit they could ever become a target in the war, the only thing standing between them and total annihilation was First Fleet.

A muffled explosion dragged Ashlyn's attention back to the building. Boomer's voice came over the comm, reporting breach had been made. Ashlyn grinned and stood. It was time to pay Alexander Watchman a visit. If there was any justice in the universe, he'd be waiting for them.

---

WATCHMAN GRABBED for a handhold as the entire building shook. Dust dropped from the ceiling, filling the air. From the other room, alarms sounded. He stood where he was, body tense, as he waited for the second explosion. Could the Callusians be attacking already?

Fear building, he looked around. His mind raced but in too many directions, making it almost impossible to focus. He closed his eyes and fought for control. He needed to be calm, to think. First things first.

He drew a deep breath, held it and then exhaled. A moment later, he strode across the room to the closet. In the back on the floor was a duffle. His fingers closed around its straps and he pulled it out. Inside rested a clean comm-link as well as weapons and a rebreather. The latter might not give him much protection if the biotoxin were released but something was better than nothing. All he had to do was get to a safe room and he knew exactly where the closest one was. That's why he had the weapons. If anyone remained at the embassy, they wouldn't be trouble for long.

He threw the duffle's longest strap over his head and slung the bag across his back. With the rebreather attached to his belt, he picked up his side arm and strapped it to his left thigh. He lifted the pulse rifle in his hands. With one last look around the room, he moved to the far wall. Hidden next to the ratty bookshelf was a keypad. He entered a quick command and waited, praying the blast hadn't damaged the system's electronics.

"Going somewhere?" a woman asked from behind him.

He spun, the pulse rifle lifting to his shoulder. Then he saw them. Five armed and armored Fuerconese Marines. All with weapons aimed at him. Even as his brain screamed at him to do something, anything, he hesitated. That was all the woman needed.

"I've been waiting to do this for a very long time," she said just before she pulled the trigger and the world went dark.

# 18

ASHLYN LIFTED HER LEFT FIST AND DROPPED TO A KNEE. BEHIND HER, the others followed suit. Knowing they had her covered, she inched around the corner and down the hallway. If their information was good, Watchman would be in the rooms at the end of the hallway. All they had to do was make entry without him springing any kind of trap on them.

She flipped through the various filters on her helmet, studying the HUD. So far, so good. The infrared showed one person in the rooms. Nothing else showed that caused her alarm. Now to make entry without alerting him any more than the explosion below would have.

She crept back and motioned toward the door, using hand signals to pass on her orders. Once each of the squad signaled their understanding, Ash nodded. Then she climbed to her feet. They didn't have any time to waste.

Ignoring Anisimova's warning hiss, Ash took the lead. Once at the door, she watched as Boomer forsook his beloved explosives and manipulated the lock. There was an audible click a few moments later, He glanced at Ash and nodded. She pounded a fist on his shoulder and gave him a jerk of her head, motioning him back. As he complied, she reached out, her gloved hand carefully, silently opening the door.

Inside, she stood still, listening. From her side, Anisimova signaled for the squad to split up and search the rooms. Despite their armor, the Marines moved almost silently, clearing the front room and moving on to the next.

Ash moved down a short hallway to the back room. A sound, little more than the soft scrape of cloth against cloth, reached her. She signaled for Anisimova to stand still. Then she cocked her head, listening. One corner of her mouth lifted as more sounds reached her. Someone was moving around on the other side of the door. There was a sense of urgency to their movements, not unreasonable given the current situation.

Without warning, she lifted her right leg and aimed a kick at the door. As it swung open, she rushed in. Across the room, a slightly overweight man stood with his back to them. His hand hovered over what looked like a control pad. A duffle was slung across his back and she saw the pulsar at his thigh. A crack appeared in the far wall. They'd arrived none too soon.

"Going somewhere?" she asked.

The man spun toward them and she smiled triumphantly. As she did, the rest of the squad joined them. The sounds of weapons being drawn and readied filled the small room. She slid her battle rifle into the scabbard across her back and pulled her sidearm.

"I've been waiting to do this for a long time."

Her finger squeezed the trigger. The man looked startled and then he collapsed to the floor. Hound stepped forward, kicking Watchman's rifle away. As he did, Anisimova stepped in front of Ash and reached for her weapon.

"Angel?"

Ash smiled, knowing the woman worried she'd killed the man. "Don't worry, Durga. It was on a low charge. He'll wake up hurting like hell but that's all." She turned her attention to Hound. "Search him and strip him. Then secure him and get him to the transport."

Anisimova blew out a breath and then shook her head before handing Ash's gun back. "Speed, we're on our way out," she radioed the transport's driver.

"Grab anything that looks like it might be of interest to Khan and his team," Ash ordered. Then she turned and started out of the room. As she did, she radioed the flagship.

"Talk to me, Angel," Tremayne said.

Ashlyn frowned to hear the tension in the Admiral's voice. "We have the package, ma'am, and are headed back."

"How long before you get to the shuttles?"

"Racer, how long?" she asked on another channel.

"If you don't mind me plowing a few new roads, five minutes, seven at the most."

Assuming, Ash knew, they didn't have to fight the panicked crowd. Even so, she relayed the information to Tremayne.

"Not enough time." Anguish filled the admiral's voice. "Get back to the embassy and bunker down. I don't give a damn about the Midlothian prisoners. They can stay where they are and take their chances. That's the fate they signed for their citizens. But take Watchman with you. If we manage to live through the next few hours, I look forward to dealing with him myself."

"Aye, Admiral." She watched as Watchman, stripped to his underwear, his hands secured behind his back, was all but dragged out of the back room. "We're on the move, ma'am. I'll report in when we reach the embassy."

"God's speed, Colonel."

"And fair winds, Admiral." She ended the comm and prayed this wasn't her last discussion with the woman who had been friend and mentor for so long. o

---

"TALK TO ME, RAOUL." Miranda Tremayne stepped onto the flag bridge from her ready room and looked around. Her flag captain stood in front of the plot, studying the enemy's latest position. Then he turned, his expression grim.

"The enemy made a slight course correction ninety seconds ago,

185

ma'am," Kohler said. "New heading places them on a direct course for the capital. No question about it."

"Any word from Major Khan about groundside defenses?"

"He reports he and his team are in the system and have locked out local control."

At least that was good news.

"All right. Signal Captain Earhardt. Once the enemy reaches point gamma, he is to move in at best military speed."

"Roger that."

"Time to weapons' range?"

"They will be within the outer ranges of our weapons envelope in two minutes, forty-seven seconds, Admiral," the sensors officer answered.

"Very good. Comm Captain Adamson and ask her to report to the flag bridge. It's time we move out to greet our visitors properly."

And heaven help them all. This might just be the shortest battle she'd ever fought, especially if Ashlyn's intel was correct and the Callusians were carrying torpedoes weaponized with the biotoxin.

"Open channel to the fleet," she said as she took her place in the command chair.

"Admiral." The comms officer nodded to let her know the channel was open.

"This is Admiral Tremayne. The enemy has failed to respond to our hails and has made a course correction, putting it on a direct trajectory to the capital. Alpha Protocol is now in effect. I repeat, Alpha Protocol is now in effect. We are going to take this battle to the enemy and avenge their attacks on our allied systems. Department heads, confirm status. The first barrage will be away in less than two minutes. Tremayne out."

"Weapons ready, Admiral," Lt. Mardelle said.

"Countermeasures ready as well," Lt. Arens reported.

"Captain Kohler, issue the order. First volley away in sixty seconds. LACs to launch immediately after."

"Aye, Admiral." He relayed the order to the rest of the fleet.

She glanced at him and smiled slightly. They hadn't served

together for long, but she'd come to respect his ability very quickly. She also understood he knew their chances of getting out of this alive as we all she did.

"Let's get this done, ladies and gentlemen. You are the best FleetCom has to offer. It's time we show the enemy we will take no quarter and their biotoxin doesn't scare us."

Even if it did scare her witless. That was the one thing she'd never admit to anyone under her command.

---

"Go, go, go!" Ash ordered as she leapt from the transport.

Over the battlenet, she listened as reports from the battle came in. LACs engaged the enemy's leading elements. So far, the enemy was not close enough to use their torpedoes against First Fleet, but it was only a matter of time. That meant the planet wouldn't be safe for much longer. She did not want to be caught outside when the first missiles hit.

With Anisimova all but dragging her toward the building, she looked over her shoulder, making sure the rest of the squad had gotten out of the transport. Part of her felt guilty for leaving the four prisoners at the government house. The holding area they were secured in wouldn't keep them safe if the biotoxin was released into the atmosphere. But there was nothing she could do about that now. She had her orders and it was her duty to obey them.

"Mr. Secretary, status update," she radioed as they raced into the building. She watched as two of the squad closed and barred the doors. Then she led them through the lobby toward the stairs. At least Watchman was no longer bellyaching about being a prisoner. Of course, the gag Boomer had stuffed in his mouth might be why.

"What's our status, Colonel?" Nelms asked in return.

She quickly told him what she could. As they entered the stairwell, she motioned for that door to be secured. Then she took the lead, guiding them deep below the foundations. As she did, she wondered how long it would be before they climbed the stairs upward once again.

"What are you going to do with your prisoner?"

"We'll secure him in one of the rooms outside the safe rooms, sir. He'll survive if we do." She tried not to think about what might happen if the biotoxin was released. "I'm sure Major Khan won't mind keeping him company."

Nelms chuckled softly. "I wouldn't mind having a short *discussion* him with myself."

"I promise you'll have as much time with him as you like when this is over, sir." She shouldered the door at the bottom of the stairs open and stepped out of the stairwell. As Hound emerged with Watchman in tow, she pointed to the room she wanted the former Intelligence Czar secured in. "How is everyone in with you, sir?"

"We're fine, Colonel. Don't worry about us. What's the situation topside?"

"About like you'd expect, sir. Even if the enemy doesn't manage to get any torpedoes through planetary defenses, there will be deaths as people panic. They weren't ready for this, thanks to their government."

"And that is something we will make sure is addressed when we return to Fuercon, Colonel. You have my word."

"Thank you, sir." She moved into the room outside the safe room checked the outer seals. Everything looked intact. Hopefully, it would be enough to keep those inside safe if the worst happened. "We're outside the safe room now, sir. I need to report in to Admiral Tremayne. Then we get to wait."

"Then let's hope this is a short wait, Colonel, because I have no intention of spending the rest of my life in these two rooms."

She chuckled softly and ended the comm. Then she nodded in appreciation as Anisimova handed her a cup of coffee. "Thanks. Let everyone know they can lose their helmets for the moment. I want two of our people in with Watchman at all times. Room to be sealed from the outside. We'll rotate out in two-hour intervals as long as we can. Everyone else is to be in here. This room will be sealed from the inside. Tell Major Khan that one of the two in with Watchman can be one of his team. I have no problem at all with them starting the inter-rogation right away."

"Understood." Anisimova stopped at the door. "He'll want to know if you want him to move his equipment in here."

It would make it an even tighter fit but Ash saw no way around it. "I do."

The master sergeant nodded and passed on her orders. As she did, Ash sat behind the desk and activate the comm. Part of her hesitated, knowing the very real possibility that Tremayne wouldn't be able to accept her message. God, she felt useless. She should be onboard the flagship, helping with the fight.

Half an hour later, Ashlyn looked up and frowned. Deep as they were beneath the surface, she couldn't actually hear what might be happening topside. Even so, she felt like something had. When she checked the various video feeds, she cursed softly. A number of people, some civilians but others wearing the uniform of capital secu-rity, pushed at the gates outside the embassy. They were panicking. As one, they flinched. Some ducked and looked for cover. In the distance, smoke rose high in the air. At least one missile had broken through Tremayne's defenses.

"Helmet up!" she ordered and Anisimova quickly relayed the order to those not in the room. "Mr. Nelms, get everyone into the respira-tors. At least one missile has hit the city. We don't know if it carried the biotoxin, but we aren't going to take any chances."

The man acknowledged her order and softly wished her and her Marines good luck.

"Get those in with Watchman back here. We're going to seal up the best we can."

"And Watchman?" Anisimova asked.

"Leave him." She might have to pay the price later for willingly leaving a prisoner in a dangerous situation, but she didn't care. It was going to be hard enough to keep her own people alive. She didn't need to worry about the former Intelligence Czar trying something and possibly getting them all killed in the process.

Less than a minute later, she watched the video stream from the office where Watchman was being held as his guards prepared to leave. The man, no longer gagged, demanded to know where they were going. Instead of answering, Boomer turned the single screen in the room so Watchman could see the display. As they secured their helmets in place and made sure they were sealed, the man stared at the images from outside.

"You can't leave me here!"

"You are collateral damage. That's what our report will say," Boomer told him and Zimm nodded in agreement.

"Wait! I have information you want."

"Unless it is a way off this rock and a way to stop the biotoxin, it isn't enough." Zimm motioned for Boomer to open the door.

"Please. You can't just leave me here to die." He struggled to free himself from his bonds.

"Boomer, Zimm, turn on the room's ventilation," she said over the intercom, closely watching the prisoner for any reaction. She shook her head in disgust as he pissed himself. That answered one question. He knew how the biotoxin worked. "Watchman, in case you don't recognize my voice, this is Colonel Ashlyn Shaw, Fuerconese Marine Corps. You have one chance to save yourself. Tell me everything you know about the biotoxin and the enemy attack plans. Otherwise, you will be left where you are, ventilation flowing and the door open. Not that it will help you, trussed up the way you are. Oh, and don't think you can take the easy way out. We found the little pill you had hidden in your mouth." She almost laughed at the look on his face as he realized they'd removed the fake tooth hiding the suicide pill.

"Tell me what you want to know."

"I just did." She held up a hand when Anisimova approached. "Nothing to say? Then, Boomer, Zimm, leave him to his fate. If he's still alive when the attack is over, we'll resume our chat."

The Marines didn't say anything. Instead, they turned and started out of the room. Ash laughed aloud as Boomer stopped and jammed the door open. That's when Alexander Watchman, the man who most of the power players in the system held in fear, started crying like a baby and begging for mercy. How the mighty had fallen.

"Well?" she asked, her voice cold as ice.

"Th-th-there's a data disc hidden in the duffle I had when you found me. It has everything you want."

Ashlyn glanced at Khan who already had the now empty duffle in his hands. The intelligence officer carefully ran his fingers along the seams, searching for anything they might have missed when they emptied the duffle once back at the embassy. Two very long minutes later, he looked up and nodded. Then he held a micro-disc between his fingers.

"Throw him in the office next to the command center and seal the door," she ordered Boomer and Zimm. "Then get your asses back here."

"On our way, Angel," Boomer said. "Let's go see your new quarters, you son of a bitch," he muttered as he grabbed Watchman and dragged him out of the room.

"Well?" Ash asked as she turned her attention back to Khan.

"My bet is this was his insurance policy, Colonel. No encryption, at least nothing that would stop any decent hacker. But there's a lot of information here. It's going to take time to sort through it."

"We don't have time, Major. Find anything that might help the fleet and send it straight to the Admiral."

"Roger that." He motioned for the lieutenant to join him. A moment later, they sat shoulder to shoulder on the floor, their fingers flying over virtual keyboards as they worked to decrypt and search the disc.

# 19

---

*ATLANTIS RISING, FLAGSHIP*
  *First Fleet, Fuerconese Navy*
  *Midlothian space*

"ADMIRAL, the *Valhalla* reports damage to their central core," Kohler reported. "It has to fall back."

Tremayne nodded, her expression grim. The Callusian commander had been pressing the attack. He didn't hesitate to sacrifice not only LACs and battle shuttles to damage her ships but his larger ships as well. At least so far none of the missiles that had gotten through their defenses carried the biotoxin. But that didn't mean others wouldn't.

"Have the *Faulkner* and *Tethis* move in to screen it." She studied the plot and prayed they could hold out another few minutes.

"Aye, Admiral," the comms officer replied. "Admiral, we're intercepting another message from the enemy fleet to the surface. They are still trying to contact Watchman."

*Well, that was one comm that wouldn't go through.*

"Get me Captain Earhardt."

"Admiral?" Earhardt's image appeared in the bottom left of her holo screen.

"It's time." She didn't say anything else.

Earhardt nodded and turned to the helm. "Execute Operation Pincer," he ordered. "Admiral, we'll be knocking on their back door in just a few minutes."

"Good hunting, Captain." She ended the comm. "All right, Raoul. Let's keep the enemy focused on us. Execute Trojan Horse."

"Aye, ma'am." He sent the signal to the rest of their ships. As he did, Tremayne wondered if it would be enough to turn the tide. If not, she'd at least make sure they took out as many of the enemy ships as they could.

The ship rocked as several torpedoes struck the forward shields. Tremayne listened as damage reports came in. Her mouth firmed into a thin line as reports from the rest of the fleet followed. The *Pournelle's* captain reported a direct hit to the *Olympia's* bridge. Worse, preliminary reports from the *Olympia* indicated the missile had carried the biotoxin. Now they would see if the new protocols worked. Whether they did or not, Tremayne would make the Callusians pay for the ship and its crew.

"Ma'am, we're receiving a hail from the enemy force."

"Put it up."

She stood and waited. A moment later, the holo screen next to the plot came to life. The Callusian naval seal appeared and a computerized voice began. "This is your only chance. Cease fire, shut down your engines and drop your shields. If you fail to comply in the next ten minutes, we will focus our attack on your flagship and on the Midlothian capitol. You know what the biotoxin is capable of. Do not make the mistake of believing I will not use it against you."

"That's it, Admiral. The message is on a loop."

"Interesting."

"Ma'am?" Kohler looked at her in question.

"Which ship did the message originate from?"

"I can narrow it down to three." The comms officer highlighted them on the plot.

"They're bluffing." She hoped. "Focus your fire on those three ships. First volley of standard warheads followed by a run by our LACs. Inform Captain Earhardt of the new targets. Then get me Colonel Shaw."

"Yes, ma'am," her bridge crew said as they hurried to carry out her orders.

---

"I HAVE Admiral Tremayne for you, Angel," Anisimova said.

Frowning, Ashlyn opened the channel. An admiral calling in the middle of battle was never good. It was worse when you were stuck dirtside and unable to help. Praying this wasn't the woman's way of saying goodbye, she waited for Tremayne to respond.

"Angel, status?"

"Holding on, ma'am. So far, the embassy is still secure and our precautions have been unnecessary."

"Have you learned anything about the invaders?"

"We're working on that, ma'am. Watchman had a micro-disc Major Khan feels was his safety net. There's a great deal of data on it. The major and his team are working on it now."

"Ask them to find out if there's anything on the Callusian commander. Something's not right here."

"On it." She looked at Khan and nodded. "What's your status, Admiral?"

"You know how it is, Angel. The battle ebbs and flows."

Which told her nothing and everything. The battle wasn't going as badly as it could but it wasn't going well.

*Anything?* she mouthed to Khan.

He started to shake his head. Then he stopped when Zimm motioned for him to check something. A slow smile lifted the man's lips as he read. Then he stood and moved to Ashlyn's side, bringing his datapad with him as he did.

"Admiral, Khan here."

"What have you got, Major?"

"Sending you some data now. Not sure how much it will help, but it should give you at least a little help."

Ashlyn frowned as his fingers flew across as he input a series of commands. Then she waited, giving Tremayne time to study whatever he'd sent. Just when she was about to demand an explanation, Tremayne chuckled softly, her relief clear.

"Are you sure about this, Major?"

"No, ma'am. We haven't had a chance to look for confirmation. But it can't hurt."

"No, it can't." She paused and Ash listened as Tremayne instructed her flag captain and weapons officer to check the data. "Ash, hold on a bit longer. If this works and if we manage to implement Pincer, this fight will soon be over. Tremayne out."

"Care to share, Khan?" Ash asked as the link ended.

"There was mention of the torpedoes used to carry the biotoxin, Angel. Seems there may be a way to reprogram them on the fly."

Ash looked at him for a moment and then smiled. If this worked, she knew exactly what Tremayne planned on doing. Still, she needed to plan for the worst just in case.

"You and your people keep at it. And good work. Durga, make sure everyone's had food and drink. We're going to be doing a bit of cleanup before long if all goes as planned."

God, let this work.

---

COMMANDER DIOGO FRYXELL paced the bridge. As he did, he kept watch on the plot. The Fuerconese commander had been better than expected. He'd never believed the stories about Miranda Tremayne, putting them down to cowards who refused to risk their necks and their crews against the woman. Now he knew better and it had cost his taskforce dearly. But he'd make her pay. Even if she surrendered, he'd destroy her.

Fortunately, she didn't seem to realize how badly his ships had been hit. If he could keep up the illusion just a bit longer, he'd be victorious. Even now, the torpedoes carrying the biotoxin were being loaded into the guns. Once they had, they'd be sent on a trajectory to Tremayne's ship. With her fleet crippled, he could then turn his attention to the traitors on Midlothian.

"Commander, perimeter alert!" the scanners officer called out.

"Report!"

"CIC reports incoming missiles."

What? It didn't make any sense. There was no way Tremayne's missiles could be coming from that sector. Unless. . . .

Damn it! She'd played him for the fool and held some of her ships back. Now he was caught between the two forces.

"Target the flagship and fire all missiles. Then translate out of here." He dropped onto his command chair and buckled in.

"Course?" the helm asked.

"Anywhere but here."

"Missiles away."

"Then get us out of here. We can come back later and deal with the Midlothians."

"Incoming!" the scanners officer called out again.

The blood drained from Fryxell's face as he looked at the plot. It was a sea of red ahead and behind his ships. Each red dot indicated missiles heading in his direction. There was no way his defenses could counter all of them. Hell, they couldn't counter half of them. His ships would be decimated before they could translate out of the system. But at least the biotoxin would do its work. He could go to his death knowing that.

"Sir, the weapons master is reporting a problem," Comms said.

"What?"

"It's the carrier missiles, sir."

Before he could ask for clarification, the one alarm he'd never expected to hear sounded. He leaned back, knowing there was nothing he could do. It was already too late. But he wouldn't die screaming for help. He wouldn't beg for assistance from the enemy. He wouldn't give them that satisfaction.

His right hand moved forward and he punched in a command. Then he closed his eyes. This was supposed to be his chance to prove he deserved to take Dadd's place in the naval hierarchy. Instead, he had failed as ignominiously as had the Navarch.

Damn the Fuerconese.

# 20

---

Ashlyn watched as the prisoners were escorted off the shuttle. At least they'd quit their threats and, at least in Reyes' case, pleas for mercy. They knew what waited for them if they remained on Midlothian. She'd made sure, with assistance from Admiral Tremayne and Secretary of State Nelms, that the remaining members of the government—not to mention the public—were well aware of their crimes against their home system. To remain in Caspian Bay or anywhere else in the system would be to sign their death warrants and they knew it.

Now, under armed escort, Alexander Watchman and his co-conspirators from the Administrative Bureau were escorted across the bay. There would be no escape now. She'd make sure of it. They owed Fuercon and her allies for every death and injury suffered at the hands of the Callusians. Besides, she had a feeling Watchman had information she wanted. The only question was how to get it.

No, she corrected. The question was how to get it without the powers that be making some sort of deal with him that would let him regain his freedom.

"Glad to have you back onboard, Colonel," Lt. Connery said as they stepped onto the lift a few moments later.

"Glad to be back." And she was. Never again did she want to be caught dirtside while the rest of her command fought overhead. At least not unless she was doing some fighting of her own. Cowering underneath the surface was not for her. "Report?"

"Captain Adamson is waiting to brief you. But the basics are we took heavy losses to the LACs and battle shuttles. They bore the initial brunt of the enemy attack. Where we got lucky there is most of the losses are material and not human. You should have a full AAR from the flight captain in your queue."

Ashlyn nodded. She hated feeling relieved because any loss of life was too much. But it could have been worse, so much worse.

"Give me the big picture, Faith." The lift stopped and the door slid open. They stepped off. As they did, Ash frowned and her stomach did a slow roll. Even though damage control teams had been busy in this part of the ship, she saw the signs of damage and knew what it meant. "How bad?" she asked softly.

"Not as bad as you're afraid of, ma'am." Connery pulled her data pad and handed it over to Ashlyn. "We did take a hit here, but it was late in the battle. Marine country was pretty much abandoned. The dozen or so who were here were armored up and managed to slap a temporary seal in place before the damage got worse."

"And?" She stopped and turned to the younger woman.

"No biotoxin, ma'am. They stuck to protocol and kept the area sealed until the tests confirmed it."

Relief washed over Ashlyn and she blew out the breath she didn't know she'd been holding. "And you?" She indicated the bruising to the left side of her aide's face and the nasty looking cut that ran along her jaw.

For a moment, Connery remained silent. Then, realizing Ash wasn't going to let her off the hook, she sighed. "I was down here when it happened."

Ashlyn shut her eyes, knowing how bad it must have been for the young man.

"Angel, no."

Hearing something close to a rebuke in Connery's voice, Ash looked at her, expression grim.

"I went flying head over heels and knocked myself silly for a few minutes but that was all. This and Private Prejean's broken arm were the worst of our injuries."

"And Reaper?"

She'd never admit how worried she'd been about her executive officer. MJ Anderson had made a remarkable recovery since being injured so badly in the same battle that cost Lucinda Ortega her life. But this was her first time back on the front lines since the battle and she still wasn't one hundred percent. The fact the captain hadn't met her when her shuttle docked worried her.

"She came through without a scratch." Now Connery grinned and stepped aside so Ash could enter her quarters. "However, I'll warn she is has promised to skin you alive if you ever get yourself stuck dirtside before a battle."

Ashlyn chuckled and handed Connery's data pad back. "The admiral?"

"Like most of us, a few bumps and bruises. You're to report to her ready room as soon as you've freshened up."

"All right." She thought for a moment. "Comm MJ and ask her to meet us here. The two of you can give me the lecture I know you've prepared while I change. Then I'll report to the admiral. Afterwards, I want a meeting with the two of you and company commanders. Let's see how we did and what we can do better next time."

Because there would be a next time and a time after that. This was wouldn't end any time soon unless they quit playing a defensive game and finally went on the offensive.

"Food?" Connery asked.

"Coffee. I'd better not keep the admiral waiting."

"I'll see to it." She paused for a moment. "Captain Adamson will be here in a few minutes, ma'am. She's making sure the prisoners are secured according to your orders."

Ash nodded, relieved. That explained why Adamson hadn't been there to meet her. It was also exactly what she should have expected from the captain. But, just as the blonde was getting used to being an officer, Ash was getting used to her as XO.

"Let the admiral know I'll be there in fifteen. If she asks, remind her—respectfully, of course." She grinned a little cheekily as Connery groaned softly. "That I've been in my battle armor for most of the last three days. A shower is very muchly needed."

"Why, Colonel, would I ever tell and admiral that my CO stinks?" She looked so innocent, except for that flash of devilment in her eyes.

"Oh, you most definitely would," Ashlyn countered. "Make the comms and I will get cleaned up."

Twenty minutes later, dressed in a clean uniform for the first time since before the fighting began, Ashlyn entered Admiral Tremayne's ready room. As she did, she glanced at the conference table in the center of the room. Half the seats were unoccupied, the officers usually sitting there either dead or injured. The battle may not have been prolonged, but the toll had been high. Almost too high. Even so, Ash knew it could have been much worse.

"My apologies for being late, Admiral," she said as she took her seat.

"No need, Colonel, I understand."

Ash knew she did, which made it easier. At least in some ways.

"Have a seat, Colonel. We've a great deal to cover." Tremayne waited as Ashlyn complied. At the same time, several junior ratings poured coffee and set out plates of sandwiches for those who wanted them. The admiral waited until the three left the ready room and the hatch slid shut behind them before continuing.

"Before we get into everyone's after-action reports, I wanted to confirm what most of you have probably already heard. Colonel Shaw and her team not only managed to take Alexander Watchman into custody, but they also exposed several members of the Administrative Bureau and they have been arrested as well. Secretary of State Nelms and Ambassador Izaguirre worked with the Midlothian judiciary and secured orders turning each of the prisoners over to us for transport back to Fuercon. There they will be prosecuted for their crimes against our system. Then our allies will have a chance at them. When that is all done and their sentences served, assuming they don't face execution for their crimes, they will be returned to Midlothian to face judgment there.

"Major Khan and his people will continue questioning them. They will be appointed advocates to help protect their rights." Tremayne shook her head, stopping any objections. "That is their right under our own laws. We will not sink to their levels, no matter how tempting it might be. Understood?" She waited until everyone gathered assured her that they did.

"However, they are being considered enemy combatants because of their actions. That means their legal rights are limited. They won't be harmed. They won't be threatened, except with the possible penalties they face when convicted. Colonel Shaw, your Marines have the security duty."

"Understood, ma'am." She assumed they would based on the few minutes she had with Anderson prior to reporting to the ready room. "Captain Anderson is setting it up as we speak. She's had the prisoners placed in separate cells, far enough apart they can't communicate with one another. There are some concerns, legitimate in my mind, about at least one of the prisoners attempting suicide. So I've ordered guards posted outside each cell and constant video monitoring."

"Very good. Keep me informed." Tremayne glanced at her notes. "Now, Colonel, I want to commend your Marines. They performed above and beyond during the battle. I know how difficult it was for you to be stuck dirtside. I'd have hated it had I been in your position. But you've trained them better than any Navy CO could hope for. I know they helped save lives."

"Thank you, ma'am. I'll be sure to pass your compliments on to Captain Anderson. She did all the hard work."

Tremayne chuckled and shook her head. "I know you, Ash. You had the hard job. Or maybe I should say Master Sergeant Anisimova did trying to keep you from grabbing a shuttle and hightailing it back here so you'd be in the middle of the action."

Ash's cheeks heated and she shrugged. What else could she do? Especially since she had considered doing just that more than once.

"There is one more thing before we begin the AARs." Tremayne sipped her coffee before continuing. "We have received new orders. FleetCom has dispatched our relief. Once it is here, we are to return to Fuercon. In the meantime, we are to proceed with repairs and with making sure the Midlothians understand they have to become a true ally if they want our protection to continue. Ambassador Izaguirre and his staff will return to the surface to resume their duties. We are to transport any dependents and others who wish to return back to Fuercon.

"Once home, our prisoners will be removed into Fleet Intel's custody. As soon as our repairs are finalized and replacement personnel and material are in place, we will leave the system. From there we will go at best military speed to rendezvous with the leading elements of the final push. President Harper has made it clear. We are ending this war and, to do so, we will take the fight straight to the Callusians." Tremayne stood, her expression fierce.

"Ladies and gentlemen, in very short order, we are going to make the enemy pay for all it has done to us and to our allies. We will not let them hold the threat of the biotoxin over us or any other system.

"President Harper and FleetCom send their congratulations on a mission well done and ask us to do the same with our ultimate goal. The Callusian home system. What say you?"

Ash stood and said the only thing she could.

"Ooh-rah!"

Now they had the cleanup, something that had to be done before they could return home. At least reinforcements were coming. Hopefully, they'd be able to hold the system until then.

www.ingramcontent.com/pod-product-compliance
Lightning Source LLC
Chambersburg PA
CBHW022100170626
46808CB00002B/518